# A GAME FOR FOOLS

Murda (RVC)

**author**HOUSE®

*AuthorHouse™*
*1663 Liberty Drive*
*Bloomington, IN 47403*
*www.authorhouse.com*
*Phone: 833-262-8899*

*Published by AuthorHouse  12/17/2020*

*ISBN: 978-1-6655-1139-1 (sc)*
*ISBN: 978-1-6655-1140-7 (hc)*
*ISBN: 978-1-6655-1143-8 (e)*

*Library of Congress Control Number: 2020925137*

*Print information available on the last page.*

# CONTENTS

# SUMMER 2008

# CHAPTER 1

SNACKS RINGS THE doorbell twice of the old white house. As he waits for someone to answer, he looks back to the car and motions for Tone to roll the passenger window down. As the window comes down he yells, *"A yo, roll something up while I'm in here talking to Bra moms."*

Tone screams back over the music, *"you only droppin off some money, you shouldn't be that long. Hurry up. Don't have me sittin out here that long. You know I'm dirty."*

*"I got you – just roll up."* Snacks replied with a hint of aggravation in his voice. As Snacks turns around, the mother of his long-time friend Reese is standing in the doorway of the old house with her hand on her hip. For Ms. Cain to have been an older woman she looked good. She had wide hips and a set of double D's that still somehow sat up without a bra in her old age. One look at Ms. Cain and you had to think about the saying. {The wine gets better with time.}

*"Boy come in here out of that hot sun and give your second mother a hug,"* she demanded with a huge smile on her face. *"I ain't seen you in a whole year."*

*"I know Ma, I had to go away for a while. Things got a little hectic, if you know what I mean,"* Snack informed her as they release from the tight embrace. Snacks always came through and made sure Reese's mother was okay. They were like brothers and had been that way since they were kids. What made their friendship so special was they were both from Down Neck, the bottom section of Newark, also known as Down Bottom. But they were from different projects, Snacks being from Riverview Court and Reese being from Hyatt Court. This put a strain on their friendship because both hoods would beef hard. If the Hyatt crew caught someone from Riverview out bounds, they'd jump him and vice versa. But if Snacks was the one who was out of bounds and Reese was there, it was hands off and Snacks would do the same for him.

As time went on, the two stayed close and their bond would become unbreakable. Eventually, the Hyatt crew became an official Crip set, which only brought on a heap of trouble for the outsiders of that neighborhood and the members of the gang itself because as the violence grew in the neighborhood, so did the fear in people who lived there. It wasn't long before the Feds came in and did a sweep and took most of the Crips away. Some stood tall when it was time to do the time, while others ran their mouth and told everything they knew. During this event, Reese took a plea of 144 months and was sentenced to the Federal Bureau of Prisons. This is what led to Snacks being Reese's mother's only support.

As they headed to the kitchen, the phone rang. *"Grab the phone off the table. That's most likely him. He's been calling all day to see if you made it here yet. I liked it better when he only had 300 minutes a month in prison. He done made it to that halfway house and don't know how to act,"* she says while shaking her head in an unapprovingly way.

*"Yo!"* Snacks hollers into the phone.

*"Don't be answering my phone like that,"* Ms. Cain yelled.

*"My bad, Ma. Yo what up bra?"*

"*Ain't shit you know, slow motion better than no motion*" Reese answered back.

"*Shit you here now, the wait is over. What, six months and you home?*" Snacks questioned.

"*Main man you think is sweet cause you home*" Reese mimics Jay-Z's verse. "*For it was all good just a week ago nigga*"

"*You sound like a mix tape*" Snacks cut in.

"*Nah but on some real shit, I hear you out there wildin.*"

"*I do what I can,*" Snacks replied boastfully.

"*Nah bra, that ain't it. I need you out there when I get there. We got shit to do and you need to be around*" Reese reminds him.

"*I got you bra. I ain't going nowhere. Look, let me go, I got somebody waiting on me.*"

"*You heard what I said*" Reese replied strongly.

"*I got you,*" Snacks said as he handed the phone to Ms. Cain. Before he rushed to the door he counted out five hundred dollars and dropped it on the table.

# CHAPTER 2

"**W**HAT DA FUCK *took you so long?*" Tone screamed on Snacks as he hopped in the passenger side of the 2004 SS Monte Carlo. The black leather seats felt comfortable as he leaned back. He looked out the tinted windows and saw shadows from pedestrians that walked by in their own world.

*"Man you know how that shit be. Bra called while I was in there, thanking me for doing what a real nigga should be doing for his comrades when they in a jam, then he damn near gave me a sermon about how he need me out here when he get out. It was hard as hell for me to hang up on that nigga,"* Snacks informed Tone of the conversation he had just had with Reese.

*"Yeah you know I know the shit,"* Tone replied while inhaling the potent smoke from the Dutch. Just as the smoke settled in Snack's lungs, someone bust through his Boost chirp

*"Where the fuck you at nigga?"* Without looking at the phone he already knew who it was.

*"Damn, Sis be on yo ass like back pockets,"* Tone clowned while looking in the mirrors checking for police. Snacks just looked at him for a moment as if to say, *"Nigga don't play with me."*

*"Don't look at me like you tough nigga. When Reema got you shook nigga,"* Tone said while laughing.

*"Please, you know dick run my household."*

Before Snacks could fully finish his sentence, she bust through the phone again. *"Nigga I know you hear me."*

*"What up?"* He hit back.

*"What up my ass? What time you plan on being in the house?"* He looks at his phone in total disbelief before responding. *"You questioning me about comin in the house when it ain't even 7 o'clock?"*

She cuts right in, *"Because if I don't, you will be out there all night doing God knows what."*

Before he could respond, Tone cut in— *"Bra I know you in deep shit right now, but um, we got company."* Tone motions towards the back letting him know 2 cop cars were behind them flashing their cherry top lights forcing them to pull over.

*"Damn,"* Snacks yells as he slaps the dashboard. *"Bae I'll be in about 8,"* he lies. *"I love you."*

*"I love you too,"* she said back like she heard the urgency in his voice.

He tucked the phone in his pocket and looked over at his partner knowing what Tone was thinking. They both hated even thinking about getting caught and dealing with police. This was something they hated out of everything the world through at them situations like this they hated most. *"I told you Tone, we shouldn't never did that shooting out this car."*

*"It's too late for all that – which way to go?"* Tone questions.

*"Make a left,"* Snacks navigateed. *"Keep straight. If we could make it to 280 we good."*

"You don't think getting on the highway gonna cause more trouble?"

*"Nah, bra, we gonna be on and off before they even know it,"* Snacks said, with more hope in his voice than surety.

Just as they cross M.L.K. Boulevard and Orange Street, they smacked right into a police car that was coming from the opposite direction.

Immediately, the other cops that was in pursuit jumped out with their guns drawn. Some checking on their partners that had crashed. The others surrounded the Monte Carlo that was banged up pretty bad. *"Let me see your hands motherfuckers,"* yelled one of the officers. His screams would do no good because both Snacks and Tone was knocked out cold. The next day both Snacks and Tone were appointed lawyers who appeared in front of Judge Fullilove on their behalf because they both was still in the hospital.

They were denied bails and deemed to be menaces to society. This would lead to them both taking plea agreements. Both receiving a 5 with a 3 year mandatory minimum. With the exception of Tone not being aware of having a federal warrant which led to an additional 5 years.

Damn!!!. So much for being in the house at 8 o'clock. I should have took my ass in the house, Snacks thought about the last conversation he had with Reema. Fuck it!!! Every run has to come to an end. Imma just make my next one count," he thought to himself while waiting to be shipped to county jail.

## *February 2013, Talbot Hall, Kearny, NJ*

Snacks sits in the large auditorium looking around at the familiar setting. He's been through this process on his last trip down state. Coming through Talbot Hall was part of the process of trying to get to a halfway house. Talbot Hall is a building that housed 500 inmates. It's an assessment center where inmates went through a 90 day drug program before being assigned to a work halfway house where inmates were allowed to go out to work every day or they were assigned to another drug program/workhouse. Snacks looked around the room at all the green and white signs with different program slogans. One of the signs read,

## "Anger is one letter away from danger"

Snacks read it and thought." You damn right it is, because a nigga definitely will be in danger if I anger." He laughed at his own thoughts.

"You think something funny?" the Director of the program screamed standing directly over Snacks, snapping him out of his thoughts.

Snacks looked up and made eye contact with the Director. *"Why you standing over me like you crazy?"* Snacks questioned in an aggravated tone.

The Director went off *"uh huh you must think you tough…uh you must not know about Director Trooper, do you?"* He questioned. *"Well let me make it clear for you."* he continued on. *"I'm the boss around here. I'm boss Hog!!!"* Trooper said while pounding his chest *"and I don't care what gang you wit or what set you claim."*

"I ain't in no—" Snacks tried to speak

But Trooper cut him off. *"I didn't ask you nothing and when I do, that's when you speak."* Snacks was heated. He wanted to react, but he didn't because he knew getting in a confrontation with Trooper was the quickest way to get sent back to prison and he had come too far to go back. It was a small world and he knew he would see Trooper on the outside, and when he did, Trooper would pay.

# CHAPTER 3

REESE WAS TALL and dark with skin that look like chocolate, earning him the original name Reese' Cup. Growing up Reese always felt like Reese' Cup was a soft name, so he just went by Reese. It had been almost 5 years since Reese had been home from serving his federal sentence. He had just gotten off probation and things were looking good.

Snacks was damn near finished with his bid and Reese couldn't wait. Since his return, he'd took things to another level. He had a good heroin plug that kept him with some of the best dope in the city. All he needed now was his brother to come home and run Down Bottom while he ran with his homies from up Top.

Reese sat downtown parked in his 2011 S550 AMG deep in his thoughts when his phone rang. He answered on the 3rd ring, *"What's up sis?"*

*"Where you at?"* Reema questioned.

*"I'm parked in front of the Lounge waiting on yo slow ass."*

*"I know,"* she admitted. *"Ya brother gonna kill me. I know he pissed off. I was supposed to drop his clothes off early this morning."* She pulled directly behind the Benz. *"You getting out or you want me to,"* She questioned?

*"I'm getting out,"* Reese said while popping the trunk of the Benz. He reached inside the trunk and grabbed the bags. When he had reached for the last one, he closed the trunk and headed toward the back of Reema's 2010 Jeep Cherokee. She popped the locks and he placed the bags on the back seat. After closing the door, he leaned over the passenger side to speak to her.

*"He should be good for a minute. All you have to do is get the cosmetics,"* Reese said while handing Reema $200. *"I got him a few pairs of Trues, some Polo sweat suits, a pair of ACG's, and 2 pair of Jay's, under clothes, and everything,"* Reese started informing her of the things he brought Snacks to keep him comfortable while he was in the halfway house.

*"Thank you Reese. I don't know what I would have done without you,"* she admitted while leaning over to give Reese a hug.

*"Don't trip sis. Real niggaz do real shit. Let me get out of here. I got to handle something."*

*"Okay. Do you. Just stay out of trouble."*

*"You know me,"* he winked as he backed away from the Jeep.

*"That's why I said what I said."* All she could do was shake her head as he pulled off and headed to take Snacks his clothes. "Boys will be boys," she thought while turning up her radio.

## Meanwhile

Snacks sat on his bunk waiting impatiently for his name to be called to main reception so he could receive his package. *"What's good wit you Bra,"* One of his roommates questioned while shaking his hand?

*"Ain't shit Shock, I'm just waitin for my lady to drop this stuff off so I could get comfortable, you know?"* Shock and Snacks had arrived yesterday together and they had made an agreement that if one of

them were slipping, they would pull each other up. They both were determined to make it through the program.

*"She gonna be here. I'm pretty sure she knows how you are and what you expect."*

*"That's the shit I'm talkin bout. Sometimes she acts like she don't know me or how I expect things."* Before Snacks could finish complaining, his name was being called over the loudspeaker:

*"Terrell Benson, please report to the main reception area."*

He stopped the conversation because he wanted to make sure that it was him. *Terrell Benson, please report to the main reception area."*

Once he heard it loud in clear he smiled. *"Now that's what I'm talking bout."* He hopped off the bed and hurried out the door. Soon as Snacks made it to the main reception area, he noticed Trooper standing at the window taking inventory of his things. He looked past Trooper to the other side of the window where Reema stood looking good enough to eat. No matter how upset she made him, he could never stay mad at her for long. He was in love and lust with her.

She was an absolute beauty. She stood at 5 foot 7 with skin like a Hershey's bar. Reema was what you would call 'slim thick'. Some even said she was a darker version of Megan Good, with a little more ass. He missed that ass.

*"What took you so long,"* He questioned without breaking eye contact. She looked at him and flashed her fresh white smile.

*"Don't be mad bae,"* she pleaded. *"It was Reese's fault. He didn't get the stuff to me until today."*

*"Whatever,"* Snacks said as he waved her off—signaling her to stop?

He was upset but he really miss her. *"Did ya'll get everything?"* he continued to question.

*"Yes we got everything,"* she answered in a tone that let Snacks know he was getting on her nerves. *"You might want to try your stuff on because I don't know if Reese got the right sizes. You know everybody used to you being all fat,"* she joked hopping to lighten the mood because she knew he was mad at her.

Since Snacks left, he lost about 70lbs. He once weighed 300lbs. Now he stood at 5'11" only 230lbs. He didn't look like the snow man he once did. Snacks had always been a handsome fella but he was just a little on the plump side. Snacks had skin like an olive, covered with tattoos, a beard like Freeway and waves in his hair like the ocean. He always took pride in his appearance and losing 70lbs was a great accomplishment for him.

"*Nah, I'm good,*" he replied to Reema's statement. "*He knew what size I wear. I called him last night. I love you and thanks,*" he said while grabbing the bag off the counter. He wanted to get away from Trooper as fast as he could before they had another altercation.

"*I love you too. Call me when you get settled.*"

She said blowing him a kiss before heading out the door. He aggravated her just as much as she aggravated him, but she loved him equally if not more.

Snacks headed back to his room to finally get out of his state clothes and slip into something more his style.

# CHAPTER 4

BEEF SAT IN the passenger seat of A.R.'s 2011 Cadillac truck discussing the details of the lick they had been planning for the last week. Against his brother's word, Beef still did stick-ups with A.R. Snacks had warned Beef over and over about doing things with A.R., but Beef didn't take heed to his brother's word. Snacks and A.R. were thick as thieves at one time until A.R. started to show his true colors. A.R. was a big Suge Knight-looking, greedy, underhanded motherfucker. And he thought because of his size he could bully a person into doing what he wanted them to do. This attitude and his greed made Snacks fall back from him.

One day, Snacks and A.R. was riding around just chilling when A.R. got a phone call and decided to take the call on speaker. It was then Snacks had learned A.R. told his plug he had fronted Snacks 200 bricks, but never got paid. Before A.R. could cover it up, the cat was out of the bag. A.R. had beat the plug and was throwing Snacks in the line of fire without him even knowing. Snacks came to the conclusion that if A.R. could do this and put his life in danger, he was no friend, so Snacks separated himself from A.R. and advised his brother to do the same, but Beef reasoned. If A.R.'s fat slimy ass crossed him, he would kill him on the spot.

Beef and Snacks were brothers from the same father and different mothers. Beef was a split image of his father. He had an athletic build standing at 6"6 made him look like a basketball player. Beef and Snacks were raised in different sections of Newark. Beef was raised in the section of Newark that was called Baghdad. Being brought up in this area alone made Beef cold-hearted. Not to mention he just didn't give a fuck, so for him to kill A.R. would be nothing to him. In fact he welcomed the challenge because of the shit he pulled with his little brother.

*"We been out here waitin on ya man for 45 minutes already,"* Beef spoke impatiently. *"This nigga betta not be bullshittin."*

*"Calm down lil bra is solid,"* A.R. defended his lil man. *"Matter of fact, here he go now."* A.R. nodded his head in the direction of his lil man. Just as the kid got to the car, Beef hopped out and got in the back seat allowing the kid to get in the front. Beef never let anyone ride behind him who he didn't know. He had sent so many niggas to meet their maker from the back seat and he would not fall victim to the passenger seat. *"You really don't trust me?"* A.R. questioned, noticing the move that Beef just pulled.

*"This ain't about trusting you or not. It's about me being in the right position and in this back seat is the best position for me,"* Beef said, patting the seat on the opposite side of him.

*"Whatever."* A.R. said, shaking his head in disbelief.

*"What up big bra?"* the kid said while closing the door to the truck.

*"You know da shit lil bra,"* A.R. answered, extending his hand for a shake.

*"We gotta meet ole boy at Wendy's on West Market Street,"* the kid informed them of the location they had to meet his plug.

*"Ok, cool. When ya'll do the transaction, make him pull on the next block up where the liquor store on da corner."* Beef spoke from the back.

14

"*Who ya man in the back think he calling shots?*" the kid questioned.

Beef spoke up immediately. "*I'm the last nigga you gonna see if this shit don't go right,*" Beef threatened.

The kid turned to A.R. "*What's up wit ya man?*"

"*He good, just make sure you do your part and you won't have to worry about him,*" A.R. assured the kid.

15 minutes later, A.R. and beef were staked out on 3rd Street waiting on their lick. The kid's phone rang twice. "*That's him,*" he informed them before answering. "*Shsh,*" he motioned for them to be quiet by putting his finger to his lips. "*What's crackin Loc,*" he spoke into the phone.

"*Yo don't be talking all reckless on my line. What's wrong wit you?*" Reese scolded him.

"*My bad homie,*" the kid answered back.

"*Where you at?*" Reese questioned.

"*I'm coming out the L.Q. across from Georgia King, pull right there behind my car,*" the kid instructed.

"*Ok, cool. I'm pulling up now.*" Reese confirmed. As Reese pulled up, A.R. and Beef watched from a distance as the kid got in the car with Reese. "*Yo, next time don't be talkin on my line like that,*" Reese said as he handed the kid the bag with 200 bricks in it. Instead of the kid handing Reese the money, he looked around nervously, which immediately put Reese on point.

"*What you stallin for?*" Reese questioned.

"*Nah I aint stallin, I'm just makin sure aint no cops around.*"

The kid continued to stall.

Just as Reese looked up, he noticed two men approaching his car at a rapid speed with their hands tucked in their hoodies like they had guns. He recognized one of them right from the gate. The fat, light-skinned one was A.R. but he couldn't make out the tall, brown-skinned one that he had never seen.

Reese knew it was a set up and at that moment, he threw the car in gear and ducked low in case of gunfire. He mashed the gas and peeled off and sure enough, Beef opened fire, hitting the back of the car as it turned left on Central Ave. The car spun in the intersection where he had to hold on to the wheel tight or he was going to run into oncoming cars from the opposite direction. Reese quickly gained controlled and made a right on 6ᵗʰ Street and side swiped a parked car as he sped down the block towards the highway entrance.

Boop.

He hit the speed bump, looking in his mirrors to make sure he wasn't being followed. *"Damn,"* he pulled over. Thinking fast and quick on his feet.

*"I think we got a flat. Get out and check,"* Reese told the kid.

As the kid opened the door to check for the flat, Reese reached under his seat and grabbed a 357 snub nose. Before the kid could fully get out, Reese hit him twice in the back of the head.

*Boom! Boom!*

His brain splattered all over the passenger's door and window. Half of the kid's body was slumped in the car, so Reese used his feet to kick the rest of him out the car and pulled off. Damn, now I got to get rid of my Benz, he thought while jumping on the highway.

All he could think of now was how he was gonna murder A.R. and the dark-skinned nigga who was with him. *"It's on now—Niggaz think it's sweet,"* he said out loud to himself while turning up the radio to the sounds of Fifty Cent. He was feeling himself for getting past the botched robbery and maybe even death. He sang along; many men wish death upon me/ blood in my eyes dog and I can't see/ cuz niggaz trynna take my life away.

# CHAPTER 5

"**I** CAN'T BELIEVE you *put that sloppy-ass plan together*," Beef complained about not hitting the lick.

A.R. didn't back down. He spoke up in his own defense. There was no way he was going to let him blame him for the botched lick. *"Man you the one that was on some wild cowboy shit, don't blame me.*

*"I know one thing, I'm gonna kill ya lil homie,"* Beef promised. *"I shoulda never been doing shit wit ya'll crab ass niggaz,"* Beef continued.

*"CRAB,"* A.R. questioned toughly??? His entire expression changed. Shit was getting real and he knew it. Calling him out his name was a violation. *"Who da fuck you callin a crab, slob ass nigga?"*

*"You owl now?"* Beef remarked.

*"Watch who you callin a crab, slob ass nigga—"*

Before A.R. could fully finish, Beef had his gun to his head. *"Blood don't do disrespect my nigga. That's the first and last slob I'm gonna be,* understand?" Beef looked A.R. right in the eyes as he questioned him. A.R. shook his head slowly, signifying that he understood.

*"Good—now next time, make sure things go as they should and we won't have an issue."* Beef backed away, hopping in his car and pulled off. As he pulled off he contemplated on going around the block to finish A.R. on the spot.

A.R. was mad as hell as he saw the car pulling away. He mumbled, *"Soon enough Imma kill him and bitch ass Snacks,"* As he dialed his lil homie's number he thought out loud, *"damn, I hope lil bra good."* A.R. knew the move they just made was sloppy and the chance of Reese letting his lil homie live was slim to none. *"Fuck"* he shouted out loud while planning his next move.

Reema sat in the living room of her 3 bedroom, 2 ½ bathroom house, smoking a Dutch of O.G. Kush and catching up on the latest gossip with her best friend Nikki. Nikki and Reema were like peanut butter and jelly. When Reema moved to Riverview Court in '92, they became very close. Nikki was drop dead gorgeous, standing at 5', 5" with beauty of Laura London and the body and skin color like the porn star Pinky. Many dudes in the hood wanted her bad, but she was tied to one of Riverview's trap stars named Rik. Snacks hated Rik with a passion. Snacks definitely hated the fact that Reema could be friends with Nikki knowing how bad he hated her baby daddy. But Reema reasoned that she and Nikki had been friend's way before her and Snacks even got together and his and Rik's beef had nothing to do with her and Nikki.

Snacks and Rik weren't always enemies, until one day Snacks' cousin Ro robbed one of Rik's workers. Snacks told Rik to let him handle Ro and Rik agreed he would, but soon after that conversation Rik went back on his word and had a kid named Wasi kill Ro. The loss of Ro hit Snacks and his family hard. It was difficult to point the finger on who had pulled the trigger on Ro because Ro had recently went on a robbing spree, robbing almost any and everybody, so Rik used this to his advantage and had Wasi kill Ro.

Snacks had sworn to Rik that if he found out Rik had something to do with his cousin's murder, he would be the last face Rik saw.

Rik pleaded and swore on everything he could think of that he had nothing to do with Ro's murder. 2 weeks after Ro's murder, Snacks was locked up for a probation violation. It was then that he found out the truth about who was behind his cousin's death. Snacks vowed after he finished his 2 year sentence that he would kill Wasi and make good on his promise to Rik.

Months before Snacks was due to max out, Wasi was killed by an off-duty police officer. The crazy part was Wasi was killed on Ro's birthday. Snacks felt like he had been cheated out of his revenge. Snacks put it on his life that if it was the last thing he did, Rik was gonna die.

"*You lying,*" Reema screamed, passing the Dutch to Nikki.

"*On my kids,*" Nikki swore.

"*That's crazy A.R. done crossed da line this time. He know Reese ain't wrapped too tight*" Reema spoke about Reese's craziness.

"*I know girl,*" Nikki admitted.

"*Wait until my baby find out about this,*" Reema said, taking the Dutch back.

"*What's up with that knucklehead ass nigga anyway*" Nikki questioned?

"*He good. He just made it to the halfway house. I just dropped him off some clothes and shit.*"

"*Well I hope he don't come out here on that same bullshit because Rik ain't have shit to do wit what happened to Ro,*" Nikki defended Rik. She knew how much Snacks hated Rik.

"*You know how he is and he ain't gonna sleep until he gets to the bottom of it and you know that*" Reema warned her friend.

"*Well you don't think we could get them to squash this before somebody else gets hurt?*" Nikki asked with a look of concern on her face.

"*I don't know if we should get involved. Every time I try to talk to him about it, he goes off about how he not going to rest until he got yo baby daddy's head on a platter and how he will kill his whole family to get it.*"

"*Wait, what you mean his whole family*" Nikki cut in?

"*Me and lil Rik don't have nothing to do with this foolishness.*"

"*Calm down, you know he ain't talking about you. He talking bout his cousins and brothers,*" Reema tried to calm Nikki down.

*"I'm not playing Reema. Snacks betta not fuck wit me or my son,"* Nikki spoke with tears in her eyes.

*"Don't worry girl. That nigga ain't crazy enough to do no shit to lil Rik,"* Reema spoke, not really sure if Snacks could really be that ruthless.

Reema thought to herself while relighting the Dutch. Could he really be that ruthless? Would he really kill somebody's kid?

# CHAPTER 6

REEMA STOOD IN the visiting line at Talbot Hall, patiently waiting her turn to enter the building and have her food inspected. One of the best things about Talbot Hall was that they let the families bring food to their loved ones. As long as everything was in clear containers, you were good to go. As Reema finally entered the building, her ID was checked. Next would be her food. At the table checking the food was a tall, fat, brown-skinned loud-mouth guy she had learned was the Director of the program. As she approached the table, Director Trooper spoke. "Good afternoon young lady. Who's the lucky gentleman you've come to see?"

"Terrell Benson," she said, taking the containers out of the clear book bag she had been carrying, placing them on the table to be searched.

Trooper spoke into his walkie talkie,

"Tranquility unit send Terrell Benson to Caf for his visit, copy?"

"Copy."

Someone on the other end responded, while Trooper searched the food. She noticed damn near half of the guys in the cafeteria were checking her out, the staff as well as the dudes who were on visits with their wives or girlfriends. She was dressed simply in a True Religion Jeans suit, with red Gucci belt to match the red stitching on the jean suit with red Gucci shoes – boots with 3 ½ inch heel. Even though she just had on jeans, the way that they hugged her, you could tell her body was crazy. As she walked to the table to be seated, she walked past one table and someone grabbed her hand gently and whispered "Whoever you coming to see is a lucky motherfucka." She turned around to cuss out whoever it was being disrespectful, but when she noticed who it was, she was ecstatic.

"Newarky!!! Ya crazy ass almost made me catch a case in this bitch," she said as they hugged.

"Nah, don't hurt nobody cuz its only me" he said, laughing.

"Snacks ain't even tell me you were here.

"I haven't seen him yet. We on different units. He must be upstairs. They got me on Harmony unit wit all the old niggaz," he joked.

Newarky was Reema's cousin from Elizabeth. Snacks and Newarky had gotten very close while they were down Southern State Prison. Once they found out who each other were, they stuck together like glue. Instead of Newarky being Reema's cousin, you would think Snacks and Newarky were brothers, how close they were. When they met down Southern State, Snacks initially thought Newarky was from Camden or Atlantic City because Newarky was light-skinned, bald head with a full long beard and that's the way most South Jersey dudes rocked. When Snacks told Newarky he thought he was from Camden, they both laughed uncontrollably, but nevertheless, the two were very close.

Reema sat at the same table as Newarky and one of his many female friends. Newarky was like a local celebrity in Elizabeth. The hood loved him and he couldn't wait to get home to claim his throne. Snacks entered the cafeteria wearing a pair of red and black Jordan 3s and an all-black polo sweatsuit with a red horse. Reema admired her man from afar. She stood up and waved so he could notice her. Once he spotted her, he put a little extra bop in his step.

Before he reached Reema, he noticed Newarky and all hell broke loose. The two acted like they didn't see each other for years.

"Oh shit, the illest nigga in Camden" Snacks joked as they hugged in the middle of the cafeteria.

"Damn nigga, you done lost all that weight. We gonna have to start calling you broccoli or veggie or some shit like dat" Newarky joked back.

"Okay okay okay, break it up" Reema stepped in, separating the two.

"Damn, somebody jealous?" Newarky said.

Reema waved him off as she damn near stuck her whole tongue down Snack's throat as they kissed. He got so into it he palmed her ass like his life depended on it.

"Damn I missed that" he said as he sat on the same side of the table as Newarky.

"Who's ya lady friend?" Snacks questioned Newarky about the light brown beauty that sat across from him.

"Oh, this Donna. Newarky smiled and looked at Donna. "Donna my cousin Snacks. He from Newark."

Snacks reached across the table and shook her hand. *Shorty bad as hell,* Snacks thought to himself knowing she wasn't Newarky's wife. He just smirked trying to be respectful.

Reema had made a spread consisting of BBQ beef ribs, mac & cheese, spinach, cornbread, and peach cobbler. She had grabbed 4 cold Pepsi's out of the vending machine to wash it down. "I assume I'm making you a plate too," she toyed with her cousin.

"And you know it" Newarky replied, rubbing both hands together.

As they ate, Reema informed Snacks about what she heard that involved Reese and A.R. Snacks put his spoon down and stop eating because he was vexed. He was so mad that he barely finished his food. "I'm killing that fat motherfucka this time" Snacks said angrily.

"Bra, you know I got some lil bras that will handle it for ya'll," Newarky offered his help.

"Nah bra, this is personal. I should have been murdered this nigga" Snacks admitted.

"Bae, don't get all worked up. You know Reese is a big boy. He could handle hisself" Reema said, while rubbing Snacks' hand, trying to calm him.

"Nah I'm good" he lied. Reema knew her man and knew A.R. had went too far. Snacks was heated. They managed to enjoy the rest of their visit, they even took some pictures before the visit was over. As Reema headed back home, all she could think about was the love of her life coming home, jumping right into the mix. She hoped Reese would get A.R. before Snacks got home so he wouldn't have to come home and jump right into a beef, but she knew her man, and by the time he got home, his whole crew would be home or on the way.

Shit, Reese was already out there putting up numbers. Beef was running around doing God knows what, *wild as fuck*, Reema thought. Hood would come out from hiding under whatever rock he'd been hiding under. Tone would be home soon. Then there was J.B. That nigga was another story by himself. *"I just hope the streets is ready for what's about to go down,"* she thought out loud as she rode through Riverview.

# CHAPTER 7

BEEF SAT ON 12th Street and 11th Ave, directing traffic to one of his runners in an alleyway between two houses where they sold 6 dollar bags of dope. He stood in front of the liquor store smoking a Black and Mild, talking to one of his hommies as a customer approached. "Wassup Nephew?" the fiend spoke greeting Beef.

"What up Greezy?"

"You got something?" the fiend questioned.

"Yeah Millz in the alley" Beef directed him.

"Could I get two bundles for a $100?" Greezy asked, hoping Beef took his short.

Beef thought for a second "yeah, tell him I said you good."

"Thanks Neph."

Greezy was happy because he knew how tight Beef was and for him to take his short meant that the block was booming. Before Beef could get back to his conversation with his hommie, 3 more customers rushed him.

"You got that Black Jack?" they questioned Beef about the name of his dope.

"Yeah, Millz in da alley."

"Could I get a brick for $250?" the female asked.

"You good Auntie. Tell Millz I said you good for that."

The other two wanted 3 bundles a piece. Bundles consisted of 10 bags, so every 10 bags was a bundle. Every 5 bundles was a brick. Just as Beef finished directing traffic, he looked up and noticed a gray, tinted-out Impala slowly cruising down the block. He wasn't sure, but he thought the driver was shooting him rocks from behind the tints.

"You see them niggaz looking at you all hard?" his hommie asked, confirming Beef's suspicions.

"Yeah I peeped it." Beef admitted.

"You don't know who car that was?" his hommie questioned further.

"Nah, but if they want sauce, I'm strapped" Beef said, patting his waist.

"I got da hammer on me too!" his hommie said, letting Beef know he was ready to put some work if need be.

"Well we good" Beef said, taking another pull off the Black and Mild before passing the rest to his hommie.

Reese turned right at the corner of 12th street and Central Avenue.

"Who was that you was looking at like you wanted to kill em?" his girl questioned.

"That looked like the kid who was with A.R." Reese admitted to Sandra.

"You sure?"

"I wasn't at first, but the second time we rode through confirmed it."

"So now what?" she probed.

"Dam you nosy" he said playfully, mushing her gently.

"I don't know. Maybe after we come from Reema's house we could go get something to eat" he said, changing the subject.

"You know I wasn't talking about dat, but it's cool. Imma mind my business."

"Thank you," Reese said.

Playfully she mushed him back because of his remark.

## 10 minutes later

Reese and Sandra pull up to Reema's house. Soon as they pulled up, the door flew open and Snacks' daughter ran to the car and opened the door, damn near pulling Reese out the car. Neesha loved Reese like a real uncle because while her dad was away, he spoiled her like Snacks would.

"Hey Uncle" Neesha said excitedly, hugging him around the neck tight.

"What up Neesh?" he said. Hugging her back. He always put some extra love in his hugs for her because he thought that she was going to be special when she grew up. He had high expectations for her.

"Nothing. Waitin on you to get here so I can get my phone back on. They just turned it off yesterday."

Just as she finished hounding Reese about her phone bill, Reema appeared in the doorway. "Girl, you always asking for something. Leave him alone and take your butt in there and finish doing the dishes" Reema scolded her daughter.

As Neesha turned to head into the house, Reese pulled her back and handed her four hundred dollar bills. "Pay your bill and get them new Jordan's that just came out."

"Thank you, thank you, thank you!" Neesha said, jumping all over Reese.

"Now finish them dishes before your mom kicks your butt."

"Ok," she replied, happily running in the house.

Reema greeted both Reese and Sandra with a hug as they all sat on the porch.

"What's been going on wit you?" she questioned Reese.

"Ain't shit. You know how it is."

"Yeah right. I heard about the shit with A.R." she said.

"Don't worry about that," he said as he shrugged it off.

"I know you a big boy and could handle your own, but ya boy is in there going nuts."

Snacks had been very worried since Reema told him about the situation with A.R. "Tell bra I said be cool. I got this."

She wore a concern look on her face. She really cared about Reese because she knew that Snacks would die for Reese and she didn't want Snacks to come home acting crazy. "I will, but he wanted me to hook you up with his brother."

"Sis I said I'm good," Reese protested.

"Yeah, but a little back-up will never hurt nobody" Sandra butted in.

"Besides" Reema continued, "Beef is a solid nigga." She vouched for Beef's gangsta. "A'ight Cool. Call 'em. I'll speak to him." Reese said, finally giving in.

After Reema dialed the number she waited for Beef to answer. He picked up on the second ring, "What up sis?"

"Ain't shit. I want you to speak to your brother's best friend. His name is Reese."

"Oh yeah, bra was telling me I should hook up wit him."

"Well I'm about to give him the phone."

"Ok Cool." Beef said, letting her know he would speak to Reese. She handed Reese the phone.

"Come girl, let's go inside and let them talk" Reema said, leading the way into the house.

Five minutes later, Reese came in the house and gave the phone back to Reema. "What happened?" Reema asked anxiously.

"Nothing. Me and bra gonna hook up one day this week and take it from there."

"That's good. Ya'll are the same type of nigga." Reema happily said as she hooked them up.

"Yeah, this meeting is long overdue." Reese admitted, walking back to the car.

Later that night, Reese decided to snatch up one of his hommies from down Hyatt Court and see if they could catch his target standing on 12th street. As they approached 12th, they both got point. While

Reese described the target to Ceelo sure enough, as they made it to the middle of the block, Beef sat on the porch of a blue house directing traffic to the alley across the street. "There he go right there," Reese directed Ceelo's attention to Beef, sitting on the porch.

As the gray Impala cruised down the block and Beef noticed it, he got on point. When the car turned down Central Ave, he got up and went in the hallway of the house to retrieve the AK47 he had hidden behind the door. He always brought the assault rifle out at night, just in case niggaz got stupid. And now he was ready if the niggaz in the Impala wanted action.

As they rounded the block, Reese told Ceelo the plan. The plan was for them to park around the corner—leave the car running with the door locked. Reese would take the alarm off the key ring so when they ran back to the car all he would have to do is hit the button and pull off.

"Listen," Reese continued to fill Ceelo in on the plan. "You hit the nigga in the alleyway. I'm take ole boy on da porch. Got it?"

"Got it." Ceelo confirmed as they split up on both sides of the street. Reese gripped his MAC11 tightly. He was 3 houses down from where Beef sat. Reese ducked behind the parked cars as he crept low in the street, trying not to be seen by Beef. As this was going on, Ceelo slipped in the alleyway with his hood on.

"How many you want?" Millz asked, thinking it was a customer.

Ceelo never answered, he just lifted his gun and fired.

*Boom, boom, boom...*

All 3 shots hit Millz in the chest. He was dead before he hit the ground. The gunshots alerted Beef. He rose immediately with the choppa in hand, ready for war. But Reese had him in his sights and let the MAC11 loose.

Ra, Ra, Ra bullets whizzed by Beef's head as he ducked low behind the side of the porch.

Reese fired the MAC again, Ra, Ra, Ra some more, still not hitting nothing but the house.

When he stopped this time, Beef rose and fired. "Tat, tat, tat, tat, tat."

He almost took Reese's head off. Realizing his opponent had something heavy, Reese decided it was time to roll.

"Ceelo, it's time to roll out!" he yelled while running back towards the car, firing the MAC to keep Beef at bay. As soon as Beef noticed Ceelo step out of the alley where Millz was and the initial gunshots came from he refused to let him get away. He saw Reese retreat, so this gave him a line on Ceelo.

He opened fire, "tat, tat, tat, tat," the first shot hit Ceelo in the shoulder, making him drop his gun. The other 3 shots missed. Ceelo tried to make it back to the car, but Beef was on his heels as soon as he reached for the door handle, Beef sprayed the whole car, hitting Ceelo once in the head twice in the back. The back window shattered as Reese pulled off in a hurry, leaving Ceelo dead with Beef standing over him—choppa in hand madder than a motherfucker.

Days had passed since the shooting and Beef was laying low. He was trying to figure out who exactly it was who had the balls to attack him on his home field. The fact that he couldn't point the finger had him bothered. With no one to target, he figured he just waited it out, his attacker would come back because he failed the first time.

Reese sat in the parking lot of Pennington Court talking to one of the most feared and respected dudes in Newark. He was called Stretch for two reasons. His tall build, and his reach throughout the city was long. He was known to everybody as the head of the East Side Crips; some would say, next to the mayor, he had the most power on the streets of Newark. It all depended on who you asked.

"Bra what's up with you and this situation that got the lil homie killed?" Stretch asked Reese about Ceelo's death.

"I got it under control bra, don't trip."

"Don't trip?!" Stretch asked, raising his voice.

"How you gonna ask me not to trip when you not letting nobody know what's going on. And on top of it all, we just lost a good lil homie, so don't ask me not to trip when you got a personal war going on and I'm in the dark—

"Bra I'm sorry about Ceelo," Reese cut in, I can't bring him back, but I promise I won't sleep until I put this nigga to sleep" Reese promised.

"This what I'mma do. I'm put 3 niggaz on A.R., so don't worry about him, just focus on this mystery nigga you don't know nothing about" Stretch spoke his last words dripping with sarcasm.

"Bra, I don't need help, I got it" Reese said, locking eyes with the big homie. As he looked at Stretch, he could tell it wasn't up to debate. But to his surprise, Stretch agreed.

"Okay, but if I have to get involved, shit gonna get messy" he said, looking over his shoulder while getting out the car.

# CHAPTER 8

S NACKS SAT IN the lecture hall listening to the counselor as she spoke about addiction and drug abuse. Snacks hated that he had to listen to this bullshit. He wasn't a fiend, *addiction had nothing to do with him*, so he thought. Snacks couldn't wait until it was time for Rec so he could kick it with Newarky. Being as though him and Newarky was on different units, they only got to kick it at Rec, which was once a day.

"That will be all for today" the short, dread-headed counselor said, wrapping up the last lecture for the day.

Everybody rushed out of the large lecture hall, rushing to line up to head out for Rec.

"Mr. Benson, may I have a word with you?" the counselor asked, stopping Snacks as he tried to exit the lecture hall.

"I really don't have time right now," Snacks tried to brush him off, uninterested in what he had to say.

"Well, I'll walk with you," the counselor refused to be brushed off.

"Ok, whatever," Snacks gave in, sounding defeated.

"When are you going to start taking your recovery seriously?" the counselor asked.

"Are you serious Mr. Bates? I'm not no fiend."

"Oh I see, you're above all that, huh?" Mr. Bates asked, setting Snacks up for his next conversation.

"Damn right," Snacks said proudly. By this time they had stopped walking.

"So you didn't smoke weed?" Mr. Bates asked.

"Of course, everybody smoke weed," Snacks said.

"No, everybody doesn't. So I suppose you don't drink either?" Mr. Bates continued to question Snacks about his lifestyle.

"Only when I go to the strip club" Snacks admitted.

"Do you hear yourself? You stand here, Mr. Big Bad Drug Dealer who doesn't realize how many families he's destroying, or you can't even see how you're destroying your own family?"

"My family good." Snacks was offended by his last comment.

"Oh your family good?" Mr. Bates said, mimicking Snacks. "So your wife and kids is good coming here every week, hearing Trooper's big ass mouth about what ya'll can and can't do on a visit, they good with that?" Mr. Bates questioned. "Not only are you in denial, you have what we call cross-addictions."

"What?" Snacks spat, in disbelief.

"Yes, you're addicted to the lifestyle of selling drugs, women, weed, alcohol, and God knows what else. He wanted to get into the ABC's (activating event, belief system, consequences) that he just covered during his seminar but he knew that he would've been frustrated even more if Snacks would've prove his doubt that he didn't follow the lecture. "I suggest you start to pay attention before it's too late. Now you can go to your precious Rec period." Mr. Bates stormed off, giving Snacks something to think about.

*Was he really an addict? Was he really destroying his loved ones lives?*

As Snacks entered the Rec yard, he looked around to see if he could spot Newarky. It was next to impossible to spot Newarky in the sea of people, so he decided he would walk around the yard for a few laps. If he didn't see him by then, he would go back upstairs and use the phone. On his second lap around, he spotted Newarky chopping it up in the corner with some dudes from Elizabeth. Whatever they were talking about must have been serious because Newarky had everybody's attention.

Newarky was animated like usual but he stopped in mid- sentence when he spotted Snacks approaching. "Oh shit, what's up cuzzo?" Newarky greeted Snacks with a handshake, bringing him in for a hug.

"I'm coolin'" Snacks replied

Newarky introduced Snacks to the other two guys. "This Rocky and this Qua. This my cousin Snacks."

They all shook hands and Newarky finished where he had left off "like I was saying, this Mayhem shit gone be crazy" Newarky said, pounding his fist into his hand for emphasis.

"What you talking about?" Snacks asked, not knowing what they were talking about because he had just walked up.

"I was just telling these niggaz about an idea I got for this web series. This shit gonna be dope" Newarky spoke, full of enthusiasm. They talked about the idea of Mayhem for a few more minutes than Rocky and Qua stepped off, leaving Snacks and Newarky still talking. It wasn't hard to figure out that they really wanted to chop it alone. The looks that Snacks was giving up told the entire story. He had something on his mind.

"So what took you so long to come out?" Newarky asked in between puffs of his Newport.

"Mr. Bates had me in a head lock talking this shit about me being an addict along with a bunch of other bullshit."

As Snacks recalled the conversation with Mr. Bates, he got upset all over again.

"Keeping real my nigga, Mr. Bates is one of the realest counselors here," Newarky spoke on Mr. Bates' behalf. He continued, "I took his Life Skills class twice" Newarky admitted. "Just get to know him. He's a good dude."

"Answer me this."

"Shoot," Newarky said, waiting for Snacks to spit some more negativity.

"What the fuck I need to program for when I'm going straight back to the game?"

"Yeah, A Game For Fools" Newarky mumbled, plucking his finished Newport to the ground. Newarky loved Snacks like a brother but he couldn't believe they had just done a bunch of time and here it was Snacks was about go out there in do the same thing all over again. At this very moment Newarky didn't want to kick it with him anymore. Snacks' negative thinking was making him mad so he told Snacks he would catch him later and Newarky left Snacks standing in the rec yard and went back inside the building. Snacks wondered what his problem.

# CHAPTER 9

REEMA SAT ON her couch talking to Reese while smoking the Dutch of haze. As she let out a cloud of smoke and thought whether she should bring up the situation with him and A.R. She didn't want to get right into it so she beat around the bush. "So you been staying out of trouble?"

"Trying to, but it's kinda crazy right now he admitted."

"What's good wit that situation wit A.R," she questioned?

"It's like that mothafucka left da city or somethin. I can't find him nowhere." he said, while taking deep pulls from the Dutch.

"Well I asked Beef did he see him lately. He ain't seen him either." she said while reaching for the Dutch from Reese. "I never told Beef what I wanted with A.R. because I didn't know if you wanted him to know what was going on."

"Nah, its better you didn't say nothing. I'm just meeting bra, I don't want him thinking I got too much going on, feel me?" Reese looked for confirmation in Reema's face.

"Nah Beef ain't like dat. Y'all going to get along just fine. That nigga just as crazy as your wild ass."

"What time he say he was gonna be here?"

"Let me call his ass and see how far away he is," Reema reached for her phone on the coffee table. Beef answered on the 3rd ring.

"What up sis," Beef answered on the other end.

"What time you commin."

"I'll be there in a few."

"A'ight, Reese wanted to know because he was about to leave."

"Tell him I said if I'm not there in the next 15 minutes, I'll get with him tomorrow."

They said their goodbyes and hung up.

20 minutes later, Beef still hadn't arrived, so Reese headed out the door with his phone in his hand. "Sis, I got to go, my phone is going crazy. Tell bra I tried to wait but I had to bounce." Reese said before pulling off.

"Okay, love you boy," Reema screamed as the car pulled off.

Just as Beef was coming up South Orange Ave., he passed someone who looked too familiar riding in the other direction, so he turned in Dunkin' Donuts' parking lot and came out 2 cars behind his suspect. He followed the familiar face at a safe distance, hoping and praying this was who he thought it was. If it was who he thought it was, he was going to make him pay right now for coming through his block like he was a mad man.

Reese was hungry, so he decided he would stop at one of Newark's most famous chicken spots called Ambassador's. Ambassadors are famous wings and shrimps. It is a little spot in a strip mall on South Orange Avenue that stays jammed pack. He turned in the small parking lot that was full of cars. Within seconds he eased his car into a spot not too far from the entrance of the takeout spot.

Beef parked across from Ambassador's and watched his prey enter the packed chicken spot. *"It must be Christmas,"* he said out loud as he laughed. *"My girl always said these wings were to die for."*

10 minutes later, Reese was walking out the door with his order, followed by a big butt girl with a small waste and a pretty face. He had

been pushing up on her the whole time he waited for his food. They stopped in front of one of the stores to exchange numbers. Just as Reese finished storing the girl's number, he looked up and you would have thought he saw a ghost when he noticed Beef raising his gun, headed in his direction. The girl noticed the look on Reese's face and turned to see what froze and startled him. When she saw Beef coming in their direction she froze with fear too.-

Beef raised the .357 and fired just as his prey looked up.

*"Boom, boom, boom."*

The first shot hit Reese in the shoulder, knocking him against the store, but he recovered quickly and grabbed the girl he had been talking to, using her as a shield as Beef continued to fire.

*"Boom, boom, boom."*

The rest of Beef's shots hit the screaming girl directly in the chest, killing her on impact. *"Fuck!"* He was mad as hell as he jogged back to his car and pulled off as if nothing happened. He damn near through a fit when he realized that he didn't kill his intended target. He wanted to double back and finish him off but he realized that most likely cops was on their way to the scene.

Reese laid under the dead girl, bleeding rapidly – he was losing a lot of blood and fast. His shoulder was aching with so much pain that he couldn't stand. This was his first time ever getting shot. He wasn't used to being on this side of the gun. He knew that he was going to have to get this beef over with and fast because this was something he couldn't get used too.

A fat guy who wore some beat up sneakers and a durag covering his head pulled Reese from under the girl. "Yo, man, you ok?" the man asked hysterically. "I called the ambulance—they're on the way." He looked scared because he didn't want to see the Reese die on him. He already saw the girl sprawled out—that alone had him rattled.

"I'm getting dizzy," was the last thing Reese said before he passed out.

# CHAPTER 10

SNACKS SAT IN the cafeteria eating his lunch. "Can I sit here?" a guy from his unit asked while taking the seat.

"Why ask can you sit there if you know I wasn't gonna say no?" Snacks stated before taking a bite of his chicken patty.

"Because in the pen, I would have had to stab you for not asking before you sat down," he warned with an aggressive body language.

"Oh yeah, I forgot" Snacks said with a little chuckle."

"See, that's what I'm talking about. If you forget in the pen, you get stabbed," the man said again.

The man Snacks was talking to was known as Penitentiary Flip. Some referred to him as *Mr. know it all*. He was a fat boy who thought he was cocky. He had a few muscles but he had some fat too in the wrong places. He had just finished serving 60 months in the Feds and all he talked about was…*if you was in the pen, you would've gotten stabbed for this or that*." He was truly institutionalized, but he would never admit it. Every time Snacks would point out to him that he was institutionalized, he would argue back that he was just trying to get Snacks ready for when he went to the penitentiary. And every time Snacks would look at him like he was crazy because after this, Snacks vowed he would never come back and he meant that. But Flip would tell him as long as he had plans on going back to the streets, the pen had a bed waiting for him.

After they had finished eating, Snacks and Flip headed back to their unit. As they entered the T.V. area on Tranquility they both took a seat in the back and continued their conversation. "So you really think you going out there to sell dope and not end up back in here huh, Flip said as he made eye contact with Snacks waiting for a response.

"See you think I'm your average corner boy, that ain't me my nigga. I don't have to do that hand to hand shit" Snacks boasted.

"Ok boss, when the Feds want you they gone make your so called workers flip on you, and it's gonna be the niggas you least expect it to be—

Snacks cut Flip off, "man all of my niggas solid. If a nigga do snitch, you know the campaign."

"And what's that" Flip Asked.

"K.A.R Nigga, Kill All Rats."

Flip shook his head in disbelief "Okay Mr. Know it all, just don't say you haven't been warned."

Snacks had to laugh at that one, because it was no arguing with the True Mr. Know it all himself.

# CHAPTER 11

RIK WOKE UP to the smell of turkey sausages, pancakes and eggs. He was a funny looking guy with glasses and big teeth. Everybody wanted to know how he got a girl of Nikki's caliber, but that was a rhetorical question because everybody knew he had money. He had just left the bathroom and now headed to the kitchen to see what smelled so good. As he entered the kitchen, Nikki stood over the stove scrambling the last of the eggs.

Rik stood in the doorway taking in the beautiful site before him. Nikki stood in nothing but a pair of light blue boy shorts that the bottom of her phat red ass hung out of and a tight tank top that her hard eraser sized nipple poked right through the fabric. The site of her still drove him crazy. He hadn't been home in about a week because of his latest business venture out of town and he really missed his lady. Nikki finally turned around to get some cheese out the fridge and was startled by Rik's presence. "Boy you scared the shit out of me" she said slapping him on his chest. As her hand landed on his chest, he grabbed her and pulled her in for a kiss. He kissed her long and passionately, palming her big soft ass at the same time. "You better stop before you make me burn the food" she said as she broke their embrace.

"It won't be the first time you burned some shit up in here" he teased.

"Yeah right nigga I cook better than your momma" she shot back.

"My momma huh?" he smirked "Why don't I call her and tell her you said that" Rik joked as he reached for the phone.

"You would do that you ol' momma's boy" she teased. She tried to wrestle the phone from his grasp. As the tussled, she ended up taking the phone from him. He tried to get it back but she held it out of his reach by bending over the table, stretching her arms out. By doing that, this put her ass on his groin, which led to him instantly getting an erection. "Oh you wanna play" Rik said as he slid his manhood out, slapping her on her ass with it. Before she could protest or respond he had her panties to the side and half of his dick inside her.

"Oouu Nigga you so sneaky" she cried out in passion. "Damn I missed this dick" she screamed as she threw her ass at him wildly.

Rik was putting in work on her too, but watching her move her ass like a stripper had him mesmerized and before he knew it he was yelling "I'm Cummmiiingg" then he shot his load inside her. "Dam girl" he said as he gripped her tightly by her ass. "Whew, that was the best quickie I ever had. I missed that shit" he admitted while smacking her on her ass while tucking himself back in his boxers.

"I bet you did" she mumbled as she fixed herself.

"What's that supposed to mean?" He asked.

"You know what it mean" she said giving him a little attitude while sliding his plate in front of him.

"No I don't" he denied.

"I know you be fuckin when you not here for weeks at a time."

"Oh boy, here we go wit the bullshit" Rik said throwing his hands up. "I just gave you the best 20 minutes of your life and you gon ruin it like this."

"Nah we cool, I'm just letting you I'm hip to your bullshit and you better not bring me no STD in this motherfucka or we gon have a problem" She threatened while getting in the shower. "And it was only 10 minutes Nigga" she said as she laughed.

45 minutes later, Rik and Nikki sat in the living room passing a dutch back and forth to each other. Rik flipped through the channels till finally settling on sports center. "I was at Reema's house and she said that nigga Snaa-" before she could finish his name, Rik held his hand up to stop her.

"You know that nigga's name is not too be spoken around me or in my house."

"Well I think you need to hear this" she cut back in with a bit of an attitude. "Like I was saying…Reema told me that nigga talkin crazy, how he will kill ya whole family to get to you." Rik slammed the remote control on the table so hard he damn near shattered the glass.

"That bitch ass nigga ain't gon do shit!" Rik screamed at the top of his lungs. "He all talk! He know he can't see me" He said while pounding his chest with a closed fist. Rik continued on screaming "RVC is mine and I will kill everything he love to keep it" Rik threatened. "You know what?" He calmed down a bit before speaking again. "When he comes home I'll be untouchable" Rik bragged.

"Well I hope you'll be untouchable within the next few months because that nigga is about to go to Kentock reaaal soon" Nikki warned putting emphasis on 'real'.

Kentock was a halfway house where Snacks would be granted access to work immediately, so this meant Snacks was more than a threat than Rik was aware of. She just gave Rik a piece of valuable information he hadn't known. As she read Rik's body language she saw panic. Rik sensed that she read him so he tried to calm her. "Oh so he's going to the halfway house, that's even better." Rik was faking, he lied and said that he had a plan to take care of Snacks but Nikki knew it was bullshit. Deep down inside she believed that Rik truly feared Snacks, so with this in mind, Nikki had her own plan.

## *Days Later*

It was another Saturday Reema sat at the table in the visiting hall looking immaculate as always. She was filling Snacks in on everything that's been going on in the streets lately. She just finished telling him that Reese got shot and he was livid. "I told you to hook him up with my brother" Snacks spoke through clenched teeth.

"Don't get mad at me" she got sassy with him. She continued "I've been tryna put them together for weeks now. It's so much going on right now they never got a chance to link up. But after I leave here Im going to the hospital to see Reese, Ima hit ya brother to see if he'll take the trip wit me. What you think?"

"I think you should call Reese first to see if it's okay with him. He might not want bra to see him all hit up all like that feel me" Snacks said taking a sip of his iced tea.

"I'm not stupid. I know how to move nigga. If you would have listened to me sometimes you wouldn't be going through this shit" she motioned around to their surroundings. Which only made Snacks even madder.

"Whatever! Just do what I said with your smart ass mouth. You know I'm leaving Monday to go to halfway house."

"How could I forget? You keep reminding me every day." Reema meant it as a joke, but Snacks didn't find anything funny.

"You always talkin slick Ima end up fuckin you up"

"Nigga you ain't stupid I ain't none of them niggas in da hood you got scared of you," Reema snapped loudly, bringing attention from other visitors to her and Snacks table.

"Whatever! You so tough. "You know what? I'm out" Snacks said while leaving the visit.

"Oh now you walking out on me" Reema said with tears in her eyes. "It's cool though, you'll need me again. You wanna show off now cause you about to come home. Fuck you nigga!" She yelled as he walked back to his unit. It took everything inside Snacks to fight the urge to respond, he knew if he did it would only make matters worse. Reema didn't care who was around when she got crazy, she would put on a show for a whole audience. Even though he would only be at Talbot Hall for a few more days he couldn't stand the embarrassment.

# CHAPTER 12

*2 Hours Later*

REEMA CALLED REESE and asked his permission to bring Beef to the hospital so they can finally meet. Reese agreed that this would be a good time being as though he would be in the hospital laid up for a couple days. After placing the call to Reese, Reema called Beef. Beef also felt this was a good time for the long overdue meeting.

As Reema and Beef approached the nurse station to get the visiting passes, she told him how his brother walked out on her during their visit earlier. "Darnell Green" Reema informed the nurse at the desk who she was there to see. The nurse searched the computer for the patient's location before handing over the passes and informing them of the room number. When Beef and Reema got off the elevator, Reema handed Beef his pass. "He's in room 415, you go on ahead and Ima stop at the vending machine to get us some snacks.

"A'ight" Beef said while stepping down the hall with his pass in hand. As he approached room 415 the door was slightly closed. Beef knocked on the door before entering

*KNOCK KNOCK KNOCK!*

"Who is it?" Reese questioned while lying in his bed watching TV.

"Beef!" The voice on the other side of the door replied.

"Oh shit come in bra" Reese said while sitting up in his bed in a more comfortable position. As Beef entered the cool, clean smelling room; the curtain was pulled up blocking the bed so he couldn't see Reese. "Just pull the curtain back" Reese instructed as he heard Beef enter his room. As Beef pulled the curtain back it was like everything that happened next was in slow motion. Soon as they locked eyes they both stood shocked for a moment.

"Wat the fuck" Reese reacted first. His eyes shot to the table where his .38 snub nose revolver sat under a Don Diva magazine. Instinctively Beef's eyes followed. Reese lunged forward to grab the gun but Beef dove on him like he was making the game saving tackle in the Superbowl. The two flew off the end of the bed and ended up wrestling on the floor for position. Beef was clearly the stronger of the two due to Reese's injured shoulder. When Beef finally landed on top he tried to choke Reese out but Reese wouldn't give up on the fight easily.

"What da fuck is going on" Reema screamed. When she entered the room she dropped the goodies and took immediate action. "Beef get up off of him and let em up before you kill him" she pleaded while pulling him off Reese with all of her might. Reese struggled to his feet and put his back against the wall to catch his breathe.

"This da motherfucka that shot me" Reese yelled gasping for air. Reema noticed the gun on the floor and picked it up and placed it in her bag.

"This da nigga that shot my block up" Beef said trying to get around Reema. She wasn't haven't it. She blocked his path to stop him from attacking Reese.

"Both of yall calm da fuck down! This has to be some misunderstanding!" she reasoned. "Ain't no misunderstanding, this is the nigga that tried to rob me wit that nigga A.R." Just as he mentioned A.R's name Beef mumbled.

"You Ol' boy wit the Benz. Reema looked at Beef for an explanation. "I didn't know" Beef admitted.

"Well I bet A.R did" she said sarcastically. "So what now?" Reema said while looking at the two of them back and forth.

"What I'm supposed to do? This nigga tried to rob me, shot me, got me laid up in the hospital and what we supposed be best friends now! Fuck That It's on" Reese Swore.

"It is what it is" Beef replied never taking his eyes off of Reese.

"You motherfuckas listen and listen closely! Im not saying yall have to be best friends or even like each other for that matter but trying to kill each other is out. What will Snacks think if one of yall kill the other?" They both mumbled something she couldn't understand. She continued schooling them like she was their mother until her phone rung. "See we just spoke him right up" she said while flashing the caller ID screen in their faces. When she told Snacks what happened, he couldn't believe it. He said it was some movie shit. After spending close to an hour on the phone lecturing them on the significance of family and loyalty, they decided not to go after each other. Still, they agreed that being a team won't happen after blood was drawn. Their decision hurted Snacks but at least they wasn't 'head hunting' each other anymore. They each had one mutual thing on their agenda… A.R. must pay in blood for ultimate betrayal.

# CHAPTER 13

T HAD BEEN close to 3 month since the incident with Beef and Reese and still there was no progress. They wouldn't even go near each other but they still hadn't tried to harm one another, they even ran into each other a few times in the streets and just simply kept it moving. Since being at Kintock Snacks had gotten a job at a clothing store in Irvington Center. Kintock gave Snacks the immediate opportunity to go out to work soon as he got there. One of Snacks' peoples owned the store, so it wasn't really work. But it kept the staff at Kintock off his back. Being that it was his people's store after Snacks made his arrival call he would slide off with Reema and blow her back out until it was time for him to go back to the halfway house. Reema's attitude had changed since Snacks was laying the dick on her. She wasn't so tough now. Some would even say she was a bit submissive.

"The power of the penis." Snacks thought to himself as fixed a few shirts that was out of place. He was putting the shirts in their proper place, when he felt a light tap on his shoulder.

"Excuse me." He heard a female's voice. As he turned to see who needed help the female's eyes grew wide as saucers when she realized she had just walked in on the biggest threat to her and her family.

"Oh shit! Nikki what's good? Snacks said taking pleasure in the fact Nikki was scared shitless by his presence. Her first instinct was pull little close to her side.

"Oh never mind we were just leaving." She lied.

"Don't be like dat we cool ain't we?" Snacks said while reaching down to shake lil Rik's hand but Nikki pulled lil Rik out of reach." Okay cool I see how it is. I didn't know it was like dat" He smirked.

"Snacks I'm tellin you stay the fuck away from me and my son." Nikki screamed as she ran out the store dragging lil Rik along the way. Just as she made it to the door she bumped into the owner and kept it moving right pass him.

"What was that all about?" The owner questioned while looking over his shoulder to get a look at Nikki's fat ass as she stormed off.

"I don't know." Snacks lied. As he shrugged.

"Yeah right." The owner replied knowing Snacks knew exactly what was going on. "If you need me I'll be in the back." he said leaving Snacks alone to run the store.

Later that night back at Kintock Snacks had just taken a shower and was now sitting on his bed talking to the guy that slept next to him about a female that he had met in the store he worked in the day before. "I'm tellin you she was bad as hell." Snacks bragged.

"Yeah well I hope she worth dyin for cause, I seen how ya wifey be comin and she look like she don't be playin wit you." The man teased.

"Let me worry about dat. It's enough of me to go around for everybody." Snacks joked.

"Okay I could see I'ma be comin to your funeral." His roommate joked. In the middle of their conversation two counselors busted in the room. One of them was a Supervisor so there had to be a serious issue.

"Mr.Benson Please come to the front office."

"Why whats wrong" Snacks asked looking at both counselors for a sign of uncertainty.

"Nothing's wrong we just reec a urine test" he lied. Snacks was hesitant at first something told him to kick the back door open and attempt to escape but against his better judgment he complied. As they reached the front office he noticed there were a bunch of D.O.C Officers which caused him to feel a bit of uneasiness. It was too late to escape now, Snacks was being sent back to prison for something he had no knowledge of.


## 2 Hours Earlier

"Hello is this Kintcck 3 Halfway House in Newark" Nikki asked from a secluded pay phone.

"Yes this is, your speaking to Supervisor Jenkins."

"Well my name is Kareema Benson" Nikki lied posing to be Reema. "My husband Snacks. . I meant Terrell Benson is currently being housed at your facility."

"Yeah and?" Supervisor Jenkins ask suspiciously.

"Well today he didn't go to work. Instead he came to my house to threaten me and my son's life" she lied. Nikki started sniffling and crying to persuade the supervisor. "I'm scared for my life, I don't know what he might do" she continued with her Grammy Award Winning act.

"Don't worry young lady we will take care of everything" Supervisor Jenkins assured her.

"Okay thank you" Nikki said before hanging up.

Shit if Rik ain't gon do nothing this should set Snacks back for a minute until we get a real plan, she thought. She don't feel the least bit of sorrow for using her Best friend's name to get her husband sent, yet she calls Reema like her normal self.

"What's up girl?"

"Ain't nothing girl, shit has been off the hook you hear me?" Reema said acting a little over dramatic.

"Tell me about it girl. Are we still going out tonight" Nikki asked.

"Hell yeah come and get me around nine. I need to get out and enjoy myself for a change anyway" Reema said confirming their date.

"Okay girl make sure you ready at nine because I know how you get" Nikki said know Reema take forever to get ready.

"Girl bye! Just be here on time" Reema said ending the phone call.

Later that night Nikki and Reema sat at the bar in ringside enjoying a delicious side order of Buffalo wings. Reema filled her in on what's been going on lately between Reese and Beef. "That's some straight movie shit" Nikki said as she took a sip from her Strawberry daiquiri.

"It's crazy you said that because Snacks said." Upon hearing Snacks name, Nikki almost spit her drink out. "What's wrong with you? Are you okay?" Reema Asked.

"Nothing this shit went down the wrong pipe" Nikki lied while holding her drink up. "Well don't get none of that shit on me, don't wanna fuck my shit up" Reema said caressing her body in her tight Gucci dress.

"I could have died just now and all you worried about is that stankin' ass Rainbow dress."

"Nikki whatever! You know I puts it on" Reema bragged

"Yeah right whatever bitch." They argued at the bar all night just drinking and dudes to the curb.

"Oh shit! Reema look in the back to your right. Ain't that your boy over there playin pool?" Nikki brought Reema's attention to A.R. in the back of Ringside at the pool table.

"Yup that's his fat ass" she said calling Beef but never leaving him out of eyesight. Beef's phone went straight to voicemail so she dialed Reese's number. After the second ring he picked up,

"What up sis" he answered with a groggy voice.

"Wake yo ass up nigga. How fast can you get to Ringside?"

"Why what's up?"

"That Nigga A.R. is in here like he ain't got a care in the world." When Reese heard A.R's name he became fully alert.

"I'm on my way right now, I don't care what you got to do, just don't have let him out of your sight" Reese said jumping out his bed.

He was at one of his trap spots in Hyatt court so it wouldn't take that long to get there.

Exactly 15 minutes later Reese was parked across from A.R's car on the opposite side of the street. 30 minutes later, A.R came out the club stumbling through the crowd. As he made it through the sea of people, the cold air smacked him directly in his face waking him up a little. He wasn't lucky enough to get a comfortable parking spot in the parking lot so he had to walk down the hill to get to his car. He stumbled past a Black Chevy Caprice with dark tints. He barely made it pass the suspicious vehicle when the passenger door popped open. "A.R what up my nigga" the hooded man said right before A.R turned around to only find Beef walking up on him. This caused A.R to damn near shit on himself. Beef raised his p89 Ruger to fire but A.R quickly took of down the street. Reese seen A.R running before he even noticed Beef behind him in pursuit. A.R never seen him cross the street. By the time he saw Reese, he was face to face with a Mac 10.

"Wats crackin homeboy" Reese said bring him to a complete stop. Just as A.R Stopped, Beef fired 2 shots hitting him and dropping him at Reese's feet. Beef and Reese were now left with their guns aimed on each other. As they stared into one another's eyes they both were fearless. Reese put two slugs in A.R'S head before back peddling to his car. Beef followed suit and retreated the way he came.

# CHAPTER 14

S NACKS WAITED SEVERAL days to go to court line while in lockup at Northern State Prison. On his 7th day in lockup he was told to pack it up. He was being transferred to C.R.A.F. 'C.R.A.F was a reception facility where inmates were held until they were classified and sent to whatever prison they deemed appropriate for you. Snacks hoped that since he was never actually served a charge that they would see it as a mistake and send him back to the Halfway House. When it was time for him to be classified he didn't have the luck he wished for. They looked at the accusation made against him. Even though they had no proof of the accusations, classification judged Snacks by his prior convictions and record which proved his capability of carrying out the threats he was accused of making. He was sent back to Prison to do the last 8 months he had left on his bid. It seemed like the last 8 months were the worst out of all the time he'd been doing. Everything that could have went wrong did.

He and Reema was beefing because when she went to pick up his property from Kintock, she found the girl's number he had gotten before he got sent back. That situation alone started a lot of bullshit between them. Not mentioning that Reese was a suspect to in another homicide. Police really didn't have enough evidence to prove it was him but they was on his ass. Being that Reese was hot as fish grease, his plug fell back from him so things got tight for him. He was ducking the law and had no income. As for Beef, he had a situation of his own. The shootout with Reese left 2 dead bodies on his block which made him hot too. Detectives had his hood under heavy surveillance so he mostly worked off his phone. With all these events taking place back to back, Snacks did his last 8 months damn near alone. With the exception of Amanda.

Amanda was the girl he met in the store the day before he got sent back to prison. She held him down these last few months. She visited him every week, accepted all his calls, she even sent money when he needed it. This was a dark and lonely time for Snacks and Amanda was his light. Snacks was grateful to have her in his life. She was really earning her spot and he planned on keeping her around. Reema wanted to act all crazy and obnoxious, he will give her a reason to. Not to mention when he finally the blue sheet with his charge, Reema's name was on it. She was the one whom had gotten him sent back to prison. With this new revelation, his mind went into overdrive. He had all types of crazy thoughts, it was like the walls were talking to him. Had him going to the Halfway house mess up her groove? She must have had another nigga on the side? He even thought she was pregnant by someone else and didn't know how to tell him. With all this going through his mind it only added to the stress. Not only did it seem like the walls were talking to him, it also seemed like they were closing in on him. The closer he got to going home the more it seem like the walls would suffocate him.

On the top of all that, Reema had the nerve to have an attitude with him. Throughout his last 8 months she only visited him once. On that visit all they did was argue. Once again Snacks walked out on her leaving her so mad that she promised to never come see him again. She kept her word too. Snacks max date was 2 days from now and he hadn't bothered to call her. She was beyond livid, she felt as though she'd done too much for him, just for him to turn his back on her like that. She knew it had something to do with the Bitch he had met from Montclair.

Snacks thought he was on the low with Amanda but Reema had followed her home after one of their visits. Reema knew where Amanda lived, worked and she even knew that Amanda was enrolled in Essex County College, trying to get a degree in Child Psychology. Yeah!!! Reema knew it all and if Snacks thought he would live happily ever after with Amanda, he had another thing coming.

Reema and Nikki sat in I-Hop in Jersey City on route 440. Enjoying their breakfast and catching up on what's been going on in each other's lives. Since that night at Ringside, Reema felt Nikki had been a little distant. Now was the time Reema needed her best friend's support while going through her struggles with Snacks. "Nikki I wanna ask you something and I want you to keep it real with me."

"Why would I keep it anything less than that?" Nikki questioned hoping Reema hadn't found out that she was the one who made the call that got Snacks sent back.

"It's just…" Reema paused for a moment.

"Spit it out Bitch" Nikki said in suspense.

"It just seem like you been duckin me" Reema admitted. Nikki took a minute before responding.

"That night at Ringside when you made that phone call to Reese, you knew he would kill A.R. I just wonder if it would had been Rik would you had made to end my babydaddy's life." When Nikki finally looked up at Reema, Nikki had tears in her eyes. For some reason, seeing her Bestfriend cry made Reema cry as well.

"I would never cross you like that" Reema said reaching across the table grabbing Nikki's hand.

"I hope not because I love you girl."

"I love you too" Reema admitted. "Now stop crying! You got all these people staring all in our face."

"So! Fuck them!" Nikki yelled loud enough for everybody to hear.

"Bitch you crazy" Reema said while wiping her tears and laughing which made Nikki laugh as well. The two finished their meal, paid their bill and headed out to short hills mall to do some shopping.

### 3 Hours Later

As they strolled through the mall without a care in the world. Someone caught Reema's attention standing in the line at the Polo Store. Reema couldn't resist, she had to confront this woman. As she closed the distance between them. Even in her rage, she couldn't help but admire Amanda's beauty. Amanda was slightly shorter than Reema and much thicker. Reema's skin was a chocolate complexion compared to Amanda's complexion was a caramel texture. Reema envied how Amanda's silky hair came down her back which was courtesy of her half Dominican Heritage. With the body of a stripper and the beauty of Christina Millian, Reema saw why Snacks was so attracted to her. Reema wasn't gay but she felt herself being attracted to Amanda as well. Reema walked right up on Amanda with Nikki right on her heels.

"Excuse me, I don't think you know me"

she cut Reema off politely. "Yes I do, you are the woman who has been following me like a stalker." Reema face showed how shocked she was that Amanda knew she had been following her. Reema thought Amanda never noticed her following her. Reema couldn't have been more wrong. Amanda had noticed the first time Reema tried to follow her. She wondered when Reema would get the guts to confront her.

"So you know why I'm here then?" Reema asked giving Amanda attitude.

"Actually I don't." Amanda said matching Reema's energy.

"My man Bitch." Reema screamed.

"Your man" Amanda mocked while laughing. "I believe Terrell will answer that for you when he comes which will be with me." Amanda said brushing pass Reema and Nikki leaving out the store, as she stormed pass them Reema tried to grab her by her ponytail, but Nikki stopped her just before she grabbed her from behind.

"Now is not the or place she gonna get hers." Nikki said consoling her friend.

## August, 18, 2014

2 Days after her run in with Reema at the mall Amanda sat in the parking lot of Bayside State Prison waiting on her new Boo to be released. She had really been going hard for him. She knew about his wife and she also knew how much he loved his daughter. Amanda hoped he wasn't just making empty promises while he was locked up. He never promised her he would leave his wife, but Amanda knew he was feeling Reema right now so she planned on taking full advantage of that. Hopefully Reema would never get him back after she was finished with him. Matter of fact Amanda was quite sure once she showed him how loyal she was and treated him the way a King was supposed to be treated he would never want to go back to Reema anyway. With that in mind Amanda pushed her worries aside.

As Snacks walked through the prison gates the shined extra bright as if it had come out just for him on his special day. Once he had made it through the last gate he looked at the sky for a moment realizing it wasn't a dream. A sense of nervousness settled in his stomach. Every man in prison waited for this moment but now that it finally arrived, it was a bit overwhelming. It was as if all his feelings hit him at once. He looked around until he spotted Amanda sitting in her black on black 2014 Chevy Camaro. He hardly could see through the dark tinted windows but he knew it was her. This was a big step for him, by not letting Reema pick him up, this would really be the straw that broke the Camel's back. This would let Reema know that he wasn't playing with her. He wouldn't say that Amanda had his heart just yet because Reema owned that for the time being but him mind was elsewhere.

As he approached the Camaro, Amanda stepped out looking flawless. She needed no make-up, her beauty was natural and her body was crazy. Along with a set of pouty lips that drove him insane. She stood at the front of her car in a Yellow Prada Sundress and a pair of

Yellow Prada Sandals. As he approached her, he joked "I don't know what's shining harder, you or the sun?" he laughed lightly.

"Well I didn't want you to miss me" she said hugging him around his neck and kissing him passionately. In between kisses he managed to say.

"How could I miss all this" as he palmed her soft ass with both hands. As he cuffed her ass with both hands she looked over her shoulders down at her own ass

"I know right? It's a lot back there, I hope you could handle all of it" she smiled and kissed him again.

"Oh you gon see, I hope you ready cause Ima tear that ass up" he said smacking her lightly on her ass. The fact that she didn't have on panties made him hard instantly. "Let's get out of here" Snack said reaching for the passenger door handle.

"Why don't you drive baby? I got a surprise for you" she said biting her bottom lip seductively.

"Oh really?""

Yes really" she answered. As they switch sides, he never took his eyes off her.

"Damn she bad" he thought. It looked like he wanted to eat her on spot. She noticed the hunger in his eyes and giggled but she knew once she give him his surprise he would calm down. As he got in the car and fixed his seat he took note that she had few shopping bags on back seat. "This must be the surprise." He thought as he fixed his mirrors.

"I hope you like the things I brought you. If not, we could always stop and get you something."

"Shit, it don't matter to me long as it's not a Gray sweat suit or some kaki's we cool." He joked. As they got on the highway to head home she asked him to put his seat back a little more. He looked at her with suspicion before complying. Before he could ask the question she answered it for him.

"I know you love my lips, so I wanted to show you what they can do."

"Say no more." He said as he unbuckled his state issued jeans and let his manhood fall loose. She leaned over taking his semi erect penis in her hand admiring its thickness.

"Surprise" she said before going to work. She looked at his piece one more time. "Ima love this." She admitted right before she deep throated him. The warmth of her mouth made him step on the gas a little harder than he intended to. "You got it?" She asked with a mouthful.

"I got it" he said in a high pitched voice. He cleared his throat and calmed himself before speaking again and assured her. "Nah I'm cool, I got it" he repeated again this time sounding more like himself. She giggled and went back to work, sucking and slurping like her life depended on it. 'This girl is good' he thought. She popped his dick out her mouth then gobbled it all the way down and repeated the process. "And she got tricks, what da fuck" he mumbled. He tried to warn her that he was about to cum but this only made her go harder. Seconds later he blew his backed up load in her mouth, she continued sucking until she was sure there was nothing left. When she was done she made a sound like she had a refreshing drink on a hot summer day.

"Aaaah" she said while laughing at the look on Snack's face.

"Damn girl that shit was crazy" he could barely talk.

"You ain't seen nothing yet" she assured him.

"It can't get no better than that" he disputed.

"Just wait and see" she promised. "It's a rest stop coming up, pull in there so you could change and I could freshen up" she directed.

"I got you" Snacks said pulling in the Super Gas Station that held multiple Restaurants, rest rooms and other establishments.

## 15 Minutes Later

They met it back at the car. Snacks stepped out the restroom looking fresh to death. Amanda really had style. She had copped him a pair of all white Louis Vuitton Sneakers with the matching belt, a pair of faded blue Robin Jean shorts with red and gold rhinestones. For his shirt he decided to wear a crispy white Polo tank top to show the world the muscle he put on while he was away.

"You look good" Amanda complimented him.

"Thanks to my lady".

"Oh I'm your lady now?"

"Don't play you know you been earned that spot." As she leaned in for a kiss, she saw he was hesitant.

"I brushed my teeth in the bathroom boy" she punched him in his chest playfully. They kissed for a second and jumped back on the road, this time she was driving. "Look in the glove compartment" she pointed. He opened the glove box and found another surprise. It was a stainless steel Cartier Watch and a brand new I-phone. What number I-phone, he had no idea. Shit, when he went to jail everybody was using Chirps. "Nice watch, you have good taste" he complimented.

"Yeah, so you know what time to be in the house" she joked.

"So I got a curfew now" he half joked.

"Boy you grown, I'm sure you don't need me on your back about what time to be in the house. You just spent all that time locked up, I know you need your space." He poked her with his index finger. "Boy what da hell you poking me for?"

"Just making sure you're real" he joked.

"All real baby, 100%.' With that he just laid back and enjoyed the ride.

# CHAPTER 15

REEMA SAT ON her couch with her phone to her ear, crying her eyes out. "That nigga ain't even call me and tell me to come pick him up" she sobbed.

"That's crazy Snacks is really takin dis this shit too far." Nikki added her two cents.

"Tell me about it." Reema Whined. "How da fuck he really gon think I got him sent back? Why would I do that?" Reema continued to cry. Nikki was speechless. She was feeling guilty, she knew the troubles that plagued Reema's relationship were brought forth by her hands. "I've been good to that nigga." The tears were drying up and rage started to set in. "If he think he gon just up and leave me for another Bitch he got da game fucked up. I'ma fight for mines."

"Do what you gotta do, I got ya back girl."

"That's why I fuck wit you. I know you always got a bitch back."

"You betta know it" Nikki assured her.

"I wish I really knew who made that call, then all my problems would be solved. It's like what I don't know is hurtin me. Feel me?"

"Don't worry about that. At the end of the day if Snacks wanna leave his family for a piece of ass them that's his lost. Stop wastin tears on that nigga."

"That's easy for you to say, your household is still intact" Reema replied almost crying again. "You know what? I'm done crying, fuck that I'ma call you back later."

"You sure? Because you know I'm here for you."

"Yeah I know, I'm about to take a hot bath and roll something up. I'll be okay." After they hung up, Nikki was happy to finally get off the phone with Reema. She was happy to know that Snacks was home so she could tell Rik but other than that she could care less. She felt sorry for her best friend but her family came first.

"Ma why you cryin" Neesha asked entering the living room.

"Nothing baby, I'm good" Reema lied.

"I thought my dad was comin home today?" she questioned.

"He is baby."

"So why we didn't go pick him up?" Neesha asked with a little bit of an attitude. Reema almost snapped but she knew Neesha really didn't know what was going on.

"Just go upstairs and run me some bathwater" Reema demanded. Neesha stormed up the stairs mumbling something under her breath. Neesha was a split image of her dad and her attitude was just as bad. She loved her father deeply and Reema knew she should have swallowed her pride and been in that parking lot when he walked out those gates. She was just as stubborn as he was. So now her conflict was even bigger now that she had another chick doing her job. "Damn I'm slippin" she thought as she headed to the bathroom.

Amanda finally made it home, she pulled up in front of her condo in Montclair. As she put her car in park, she nudged Snacks with her elbow to wake him up. "Oh shit! Was snoring?" he asked trying shake his drowsiness."

"Like a bear she replied playfully."

"My bad baby" he said getting out of the car stretching and yawning.

"Don't worry I know I sucked you dry" she bragged. Amanda stepped out of the car but left it running. She even slid the seat back for him.

"What are you doing?" He questioned.

"I know you wanna go see your princess."

"You don't wanna come wit me?"

"It's your first day home? I wouldn't intrude like that. And you know your wife wouldn't like me being there."

"Fuck that" he tried to curse Reema but Amanda put her index finger over his lips.

"Shshsh… Your just mad right now, I know you still have feelings for her. You've been with her for a long time. Just because I gave you the best head you ever had, I don't expect your feelings to change overnight." Her smile was to die for.

"What planet did you come from?" Snacks asked kissing her on her forehead.

"Mars" she joked. He laughed before getting back in the car. "Oh baby" she yelled before he could pull off. "Look in the arm rest." He lifted the arm rest and it was a wad of money in there. He held it up. "Yeah that's for you, buy your princess something nice."

"When are you gonna stop surprising me? He yelled out the window.

"Never, now go" she waved him off. He pulled away turning up the Trey Songz CD they had been listening to.

## 20 Minutes Later

Snacks pulled up to the house he once called home. Before turning the car off, he counted the money that Amanda gave him, it was $2,500. "Damn she must got some cake" he thought as he hopped out the car. He approached the house with butter flies in his stomach. He rang the doorbell repeatedly until finally the door flew open. When Neesha saw it was her father she jumped on him almost knocking the wind out of him. At 14 years old she was a big girl that looked more like her mother as she grew.

"Daddy!!!" she yelled attacking him. They hugged so tight that neither wanted to let go. She wanted to see him more often but she knew that his new life wouldn't permit it. "I'm mad at you," she said as she let go of him, followed by a playful punch to his arm.

"What I do?" he said playfully.

"My mother said we couldn't pick you up because your new girlfriend was pickin you up."

"Don't listen to your mother she's crazy," he said circling his finger around his ear. He missed his daughter and he promised himself right then and there that he was going to have to take her out soon and have a man to young woman thing before he had to kill something.

She didn't say nothing. She folded her arms hoping that he realized that he was talking about the woman she adored.

"Where she at" he questioned.

"In the back talkin to Nikki."

"Nikki huh?" He rubbed his chin as he stepped beside her to enter the warm cozy house that had lovely pictures on the wall. He looked at the pottery on the coffee tables and in the window and thought how tasteful Reema was.

"Daddy home…daddy home," Neesha screamed running through the house.

"Girl what's all the yelling about," Reema asked stepping in from the back yard.

"My daddy here" she yelled again."

Reema locked eyes with the man she loved for the last 14 years. Just looking at her, he could tell she'd been crying. The awkward silence between them spoke more words than both of them could put together in a lifetime. The 14 years that they knew each other allowed them to each other's weakness and strength front in center.

"Can I have a hug?" she asked. He didn't respond he just opened his arms. He didn't question whether she loved him, he knew she did. But he did question her loyalty, he also questioned her reason for getting him sent back. Putting any authority on a black man was a definitely no-no. A wound that couldn't be healed all the way, because every time he reached to soothe the bruises, it always came back with blemishes and stains.

"So you gonna just let that bitch take my spot?" Just as she questioned him, Nikki came walking in.

"Now ain't the time" he said locking eyes with Nikki. When he made eye contact with her she saw how cold his stare was, and looked away.

"Hey Snacks, welcome home" she said softly.

"Whatever Nikki" he replied coldly. "Neesha let's roll" he said heading out the door.

"Where y'all going?" Reema questioned following him out the door.

"I'm taking my baby to the mall," he said never looking back.

Neesha came running out the house "Daddy can I drive?"

"Where's your license?" He said as he sucked his teeth. He was annoyed that fast. He just wanted to get far away from the thoughts that sprouted the moment when he saw Reema. He didn't need that type of stress coming down on him so fast.

"Daddy you know I don't got no license.

"Well when you get one, you can drive. Now get in before I leave yo butt."

"You know you ain't leaving me" she said laughing and slamming the car door.


## 1 HOUR LATER

Neesha walked through the mall holding her Dad's hand, talking his ears off. Snacks didn't mind, he missed his princess dearly. He owed her more than this and he already placed it in his mind that he was going to make sure he did right by her. Before he knew it she had him carrying so many bags it wasn't funny. During the whole time she kept taking pictures of them together, posting them on Instagram, Facebook, and everywhere else she could. Neesha wanted the world to know that her Dad was back. They were now at the food court enjoying Ice cream courtesy of a place called Cold Stone when he decided that this was a perfect time to interact with his princess.

"Let me ask you a question."

"What's up Daddy?" Neesha asked taking a break from her ice cream.

"Why is it that everything you do, you put it on social media?"

"Well I want everybody to know that my savior is home. Daddy you don't know how many days I wished you were here. All the dreams and the wishes, all the crying and hopes that I get a chance to be with you. It is hard for me to see other girls with their dad and I can't be with mines. Some nights I would cry wishing you were here. But now that you are here it's like a dream come true."

He had to hold them back because how genuine she sounded she almost made him cry. He knew that fatherly love was after all fatherly love. He was happy that he took this time out to be with her because this moment made him feel like the man he wanted to be.

"You don't have to worry about that anymore, I'm here to stay" he promised. "Please forgive me for putting you through that."

Neesha wanted to hug him again and thank him for everything he had done for her thus far. She was so proud and happy that she couldn't get it out right. There was a few other things she wanted to talk about but she thought that talking about it so soon would only ruin the moment she was having. "You don't have to apologize daddy, I understand more than you believe. She locked eyes with him and parted her lips. I love you no matter what."

"I love you more Babygirl. Come on let's get you back home before I have to kill your mother."

"Daddy can I ask you something?"

"Anything" he replied.

"You and my mom getting a divorce?"

"Nah your mother and I just need some time apart."

"Why, what you do?" Neesha questioned.

"Why I gotta be the one that did something?"

"Because my mommy said you always doing something."

"Well not this time. We just need some space. We gonna get it right though."

"So you not comin home tonight" she continued to question her father.

"I got something to do but I promise I'll pick you up from school tomorrow."

"I'll take that. I love you Daddy."

"I love you too baby. Don't worry about me and your mother, we'll be okay" he assured her.

# CHAPTER 16

LATER THAT NIGHT, Snacks had arrived at Amanda's condo around 10 O'clock. After dropping Neesha off he went to check Beef out. The two kicked it about what Snacks was going to do. Snacks didn't have a concrete plan but what he did know was the dope game was calling his name.

After he left Beef he rode Down Bottom. First he drove through Hyatt trying to find Reese. With no luck he rode through R.V.C. as he rode through his old stomping grounds, he looked around and instantly got upset. "These motherfuckas got fat while I was gone" he mimicked Frank White from Kings of New York. "It's my turn" he laughed like a mad man. "All in due time….All in due time" he repeated.

When he finally got to Amanda's, he was ready to relax. Amanda was so happy he chose to spend his first night home with her. She knew he wanted to spend time with his daughter, so for him to come home to her meant that she was doing her job. She was hoping he fell for her as she had fallen for him. At first, her father told her he wanted her to get Snacks to join his organization by all means. The visits and all the money orders all were just business but over the last 8 months, she started to fall for him hard.

Amanda's father is an important man in the drug world. When he did his homework and found out that Newark would be very lucrative for him. He researched and found out that Snacks was very influential in the city and had a mean hustle. He decided he wanted him on his team at any cost. Pedro knew most men couldn't resist the beauty of his daughter, therefore he decided to use her as his tool. Lately Amanda has been talking more and more about Snacks, Pedro hoped that his little girl won't mess up his plans by falling in love with him. On another note, if it did work out that way then it was a bright side to that too. Who better to have running Newark than family?

After she showed Snacks around her place, she set the table so they could eat. She made a nice meal consisting of Garlic Shrimp, Yellow Rice, Asparagus, and Red wine. Snacks wasn't really a fan of the wine thing but went along with it because he appreciated Amanda's class. As the two ate and talked, Snacks informed her of his day at the mall with his daughter. Amanda in turn informed him that tomorrow she wanted him to meet her father. Snacks agreed he knew how special Amanda and Pedro's bond was. Sort of like him and Neesha's relationship. Snacks took a shower while Amanda cleaned the kitchen and put the food away. When he finally finished, he entered the bedroom only to find Amanda butt naked in the middle of the bed looking at him seductively. They had passionate sex until the wee hours of the morning. They explored and learned each other's body for the first time. Amanda hadn't lied when she told him it only got better, her sex was amazing.

Snacks was far from a rookie but Amanda did things to him that he only dreamed about. What took the cake was when he made her cum and she squirted like a waterfall. She had just finished riding him like he was a bull which made him cum for the 3$^{rd}$ time that night. Now she laid on his chest looking into his eyes. She saw the conflict held within them. Here laid a man that was falling for a women he only knew for a short while but had a whole family on the side. Then there was his first love...The streets! How could she compete? Was she even willing to compete? Then there was Pedro, when he wanted something he got it. Hopefully her dad would back up when he realize she really loved and cared for Snacks.

"What's wrong baby?" he asked noticing she had something on her mind.

"Nothing" she lied. "I'm just thinking that I might be falling in love" she smiled. He kissed her on her forehead

"Me too."

*"I got a hell of a fight ahead of me, but fuck it! He's worth it."* She thought as she snuggled in his arms and closed her eyes.

## The Next Morning

Snacks was up early enough to take a shower and get dressed by the time Amanda woke up. Today he chose to dress in a pair of light blue PRPS Jean short, all red Nike Foamposites, and a red Ferragamo Belt. He kept it simple up top with a white Polo V-neck. She watched him through half closed eyes studying himself in the mirror.

"You look great, handsome" she complimented him.

"Hey sleeping beauty",

"Hey baby".

"Oh I'm baby now, last night I was daddy" he joked slapping her ass as she walked towards the bathroom to get herself together.

"You could be daddy again if you give me some more of this" she said stepping out of the bathroom grabbing his manhood.

"Maybe later, I don't want us to be late to meet your pops. You know first impressions are the ones people judge you by" he said in a more serious tone.

"Please" she whined.

"Get dress" he said leaving out the room.

Snacks had to put some distance between them because a minute more and he would have her on all fours tearing that ass up. He couldn't afford to make a bad impression on Pedro. See what Amanda don't know is that Snacks knew exactly who Pedro Martinez was. How could you be in the game and not be aware of one of the most powerful men of the east coast. So when he bagged Amanda he knew he hit the jackpot but what he didn't know was that Pedro wanted to meet him just as bad as he wanted to meet Pedro.

## 2 Hours Later

After Snacks had fallen to his desires and pleased himself as well as Amanda with a quickie they finally arrived at Pedro's beautiful estate in Bergen County. Bergen County was one of the richest Counties in N.J and held some of the most beautiful homes. Pedro's Home was nothing short of a mansion. Snacks admired the beautiful landscaping, the sculptured angel water fountains and the assortment of foreign automobiles parked around the house.

"This is nice" he said getting out the Camaro trying to hide his true enthusiasm.

"It's Ok" Amanda replied humbly grabbing Snacks hand, leading the way to the front door. As they approached, the door swung open. Pedro stood there with his butler at his side.

"Chu-la" he spoke.

"Pappii" she let go of Snack's hand and ran to her father. They hugged as he kissed her cheek lightly.

"My have I missed having you around since you moved out."

"Well a girl gotta grow up someday" She said flashing her million dollar smile. Snacks stood there watching their exchange and thought about the day Neesha would bring a boyfriend home, the thought frightened him to death. "Terrell this is my father Pedro Martinez. Daddy this is the love of my life Terrell." Snacks and Pedro shook hands firmly.

"Nice to meet the man who has stolen my little girl's heart."

"Likewise, nice to meet the man responsible for making the perfect woman." His comment made Amanda blush and Pedro smile.

"Charming, I like him already" Pedro said pulling Snacks in for a hug. "Would you like anything to drink?" Pedro offered while closing the door.

"Nah I'm good. "Wow this is really nice" Snacks said looking up at the high ceiling chandelier.

"You like?" Pedro asked.

"Do I like? Like is an understatement "Snacks admitted still looking around amazed.

"Son don't be amazed. Everything in life are just a grasp away. You just have to reach out and grab it" Pedro said reaching out like he was grabbing something out of the air. "Amanda do you mind if me and Terrell talk alone while I show him the house."

"It's ok Papi, I'll be out back by the pool." Amanda tried to lean in to kiss Snacks but he backed away out of respect for Pedro.

"It's ok" Pedro encouraged him. "She's my baby but she's grown" he admitted. With the permission of her father, Snacks kissed Amanda modestly.

"Play nice" she said before going off her own. Pedro and Snacks walked through the huge house, stepping in different rooms. While Pedro pointed out different things to him. Snacks loved the theatre, it was like they were in an actual theatre. Snacks was especially impressed by the elevator. He had expected Pedro to live large, but an elevator... Damn!

"So my son... my apologies."

"For what?" Snacks questioned. "Do you mind me calling you son?"

"It would be an honor" Snacks said gracefully.

"Well let me continue, I have done my homework. I'm well aware of who you are and your reputation in the streets. Snacks listened closely as he thought Pedro was gonna say he didn't want Amanda with him because of his reputation. Then he stated complementing him. "They say you're loyal and tough and you also take care of those whom are close to you and they say you're a killer. They also say a person should never cross you. Am I right in my research?" Pedro questioned, stopping to take a sip of his drink.

"All of the things you've mentioned are true" Snacks admitted. "But the most important of them all is my loyalty and whoever you got your information from forgot to tell you that I'm trustworthy" Snacks said looking Pedro square in the eyes.

"That too they mentioned. But trust is something earned not given off another man's word.

"I agree but you can trust me when I say I promise I will take good care of your daughter."

"This I am sure of so I'm not worried about that. This talk is about something totally different. I want you to be a part of my organization as well as part of my family." Snacks was speechless, he wanted Pedro to be his plug but he had no idea it would fall in his lap this easy.

"I'm honored but I have issues I need to handle before I jump into action, feel me?" Snacks hoped Pedro understood that he wanted a clean house before he jumped in head first.

"I understand my son" Pedro said putting his hand on Snacks shoulder. "Your friend Rik is your concern?" Pedro said as he admired Amanda's beauty from the balcony he and Snacks stood on. "Don't ask me how I know just know I know and now you are connected to a man who's reach is very long which in turn has extended your reach. All you have to do is say the word and Rik will be no more."

"With all due respect sir, Rik is a personal problem and I made him a promise. As you know, I'm a man of my word. So this I have to do personally."

"Okay my son but don't take too much time on this because time is money."

"You have my word it won't take long at all" Snacks said shaking Pedro's hand. With that handshake Snacks just became one of the most powerful men in New Jersey. As if on cue Amada looked up and blew both of her guys a kiss.

# CHAPTER 17

RIK STOOD IN the middle of the first court of Riverview surrounded by four of his most trusted men, P, Rah, Swift, and Sheed. They all listened attentively while he preached. "This nigga Snacks is home" Rik spoke with aggression in his voice. As he looked around at their faces he saw it didn't seem to matter to them as much as it did to him.

"And???" P asked.

"You don't get it, so let me spell it out for you so you get a clear understanding" Rik said through clenched teeth. "This is our shit, nobody eats unless it's us. He gonna come and think he can open shop but ain't nothing happening."

Rah cut in "That nigga grew up here his whole life. You think you gonna tell him he can't eat in the hood he grew up in, you not makin no sense" Rah disputed.

"I'm not making no sense? Uhh who side are you on nigga?" Rik grabbed Rah by his collar.

"Nigga is you crazy? Get your fuckin hands off me" he snatched away from him. "If you gotta question my loyalty we shouldn't be eatin off the same plate."

"Like I said, who side are you on?"

"You know what? Fuck you nigga! The whole hood know you scared of Snacks now you tryna get niggas to fight your war" Rah said as he walked off.

"Fuck you pussy! You can't eat here no more either" Rik declared. "Now back to business" Rik turned to the other 3 that remained. "Since y'all think it's a game, we shuttin down shop until Snacks is dead."

"What? What you mean shop closed?" P asked.

"Exactly what I said! I want that nigga dead. Matter of fact, I got 50 stacks on his head. Whoever push that nigga get the 50, until then nothing gets sold" Rik was heated Rah disrespected him in front of the crew. Disrespect would not be tolerated and Rah will have to pay for that, Rik thought as he left the meeting.

"Aye Rik wait up" P said jogging slowly to catch up with Rik.

"What's up?" Rik asked slowing up a bit.

"You know shit gonna get crazy once shit start man" P Said with uncertainty in his voice.

"I really don't give a fuck. That nigga gotta go! Either you with me or against me" Rik stated a little too loud.

"Look Homie calm down. You know I'm riding wit you no matter what" P assured him.

"Then there's nothing more to talk about...I'm out" Rik said ending the conversation.

Back at Pedro's house they had just finished eating lunch. Amanda was so happy that everything had worked out. The only down side to the meeting was Snacks would be back in the streets. She wished they could just live a regular life but she knew with or without her father's help, Snacks was going back to the streets. She figured with her father's help it would be better for him. "Sir I've really enjoyed your hospitality but if you don't mind I have to run. Today is the first day of school and

I promised my daughter I would pick her up. Baby I need you to take me" Snacks looked at Amanda.

"I was going to stay here. You can take the car" she said handing him the key.

"I have a better idea" Pedro cut in. "Why don't you go outside and see which car you like and you can have it."

"Have it?" Snacks asked making sure he heard Pedro right.

"Think of it as a coming home/ welcome to the family gift. Whatever you pick I will send the title with Chu-la."

"Thank you sir, you're too kind" Snacks said extending his hand for a shake and once again, Pedro pulled him in for a hug.

"No need to thank me that's what family is for. Now get going, don't keep the princess waiting." As soon as Snacks saw it he knew it was for him he walked around the sliver 2014 Lincoln MKZ loving every bit of it. "Nice choice" Pedro said as he walked up from behind putting his hand on Snacks' shoulder, dropping the key in his hand.

"Thanks again sir." "Stop thanking me and go" Pedro pushed Snacks lightly.

### 30 Minutes Later

Snacks was parked across the street from Central High School waiting on Neesha to come out. 10 minutes after he arrived, Neesha came walking out and she didn't recognize him at first. Yesterday he was in the Camaro today he was in something different. When she noticed it was her father in the silver Lincoln she took off running toward the car like a track star. She was so happy he kept his word. She had been bragging about him to her friend Keysha all day. "Daddy can Keysha ride wit us."

"Sure I don't mind."

"Come on Keysh" Neesha waved her friend over. As Keysha got in the car, Neesha introduced her to her father. "Daddy can you take us to eat before you drop us off" he looked up at Neesha and she put on an irresistible face "Pleasseee."

"Okay but after that I'm droppin yall off."

"Works every time" Neesha said reaching in the back slapping her friend's high five.

"So where y'all want to eat" Snacks questioned maneuvering through the light traffic.

"Apple bees" they said in unison. Snacks laughed because he knew Neesha had this planned all day.

"What's so funny daddy?"

"You think you slick that's all."

"Now what would make you think that?" she said as phony as can be.

"It's okay because when you get a job, you gon pay me back" Snacks teased.

"Daddy you know I got you."

"I bet you do" he smirked.

"Daddy who's car is this?"

"You ask too many questions little girl."

"You just came home and this is the second nice car I seen you driving in two days."

"You act like I didn't have nice cars before."

"Yeah you did but not like these."

"Oh so I was a bum before or something."

Neesha sucked her teeth "You know you wasn't no bum. But the cars I seen you in the last two days are new and you just came home so, what's up?" Snacks could tell she wasn't going to let up so he told her.

"A good friend of mine gave it to me as a welcome home gift."

"Shoot, I wish I had friends that had enough money to give me a car" Keysha said from the backseat.

"Enough about my car before y'all be walkin."

"Daddy you know you ain't gonna put ya favorite child out."

"My only child" Snacks reminded her.

"You saying that like if you had another child I wouldn't be number one" Neesha looked at her father and waited for a response.

"I don't know" he teased her.

"Oh you know can't nobody take my place."

"Maybe, maybe not" he continued to tease her. He loved seeing her act like a baby.

"Ok!ok! You know you will always be number one" he surrendered as they pulled in Apple Bees' parking lot on Route 22.

## 15 Minutes later

They were seated and ready to order. The waitress came to the table. "Hi my name is Ashlee, I'll be your server today. Can I start y'all off with something to drink?"

"Yes, we'll have 2 frozen strawberry lemonades" Neesha said ordering drinks for her and Keysha.

"Yes and you sir?"

"You can give me same."

"Ok I'll be right back with your drinks."

"Thank you Ashlee" Snacks said flirtatiously looking her up and down, liking the way her black uniform pants fit her. Ashlee noticed him checking her out and blushed before walking away with extra sway in her hips.

"Daddy! Daddy! Daddy!" Neesha called him a third time snapping him out of his trance.

"What Neesha?"

"You lookin all at her butt"

"No I wasn't" he lied.

"I hate to add my two cents in but you were looking at her butt" Keysha agreed.

"I could see by the end of this meal, yall two gon be walkin" he joked. "I gotta use the bathroom. When she come back order me a steak-well done, broccoli and a baked potato" Snacks said before heading to the men's room.

Snacks entered the bathroom and went to the stall. He only had to piss but he hated using the urinals because to him it always felt like the nigga next to him was looking at his piece. As he finished and stepped out the stall a familiar face was at the sink washing his hands.

"What up my nigga?" Rah spoke first.

"I don't know, you tell me" Snacks said aggressively.

Snacks never had a problem with Rah but he knew Rah was one of Rik's people so he didn't trust him. Rah sensed the tension and put his hands up in a form of surrender.

"Bra I don't have a problem with you, I'm actually happy to see you."

"Happy to see me?" Snacks questioned.

"Yeah man I know about the shit wit you and Rik and I'm letting you know I don't rock wit ol' boy like that no more."

"Since when? And why should I believe that?"

"Long story short, homeboy on some power trip shit and since he heard you home now da nigga shook. He tryna get niggas to ride wit him but I walked off. I ain't tryna beef wit you" Rah admitted. To hear Rik was scared, brought Snacks a great deal of pleasure. But he still didn't fully trust Rah's word.

"Ok so who supposed to be ridin wit him?" Snacks questioned.

"Listen bra I really don't wanna get involved."

"Nigga you gon be involved whether you like it or not because if you ain't in here tryna save your life then you tryna save his. Which one is it?" Snacks asked in a threatening tone. Rah was no bitch but he knew Snacks didn't play and this situation with Rik was a touchy one. So by no means did he want Snacks to think he was ridin wit Rik.

"Ok but when this shit is over I want a seat at the table so I can eat too" Rah tried to negotiate.

"We'll see how things play out" Snacks said waiting for the names.

"P, Swift and Sheed."

"That's it?" Snacks wasn't impressed with Rik's so called hit squad.

"Yeah that's it" Rah said waiting in Snacks reply.

"Ok this is how we gonna work it" Rah was all ears. "Since you want a seat at the table and loyalty is royalty, we need to test you. I want you to smash one of them niggas and you in."

"That's it? That ain't bout shit" Rah admitted. "Deal!" He said happy to be part of Snacks' squad. Snacks washed his hands and headed out the door back to the table. On his way back he bumped into Ashlee and she slid him her number then kept it moving like nothing happened.

"Daddy that's crazy you took a number 2 in there" Neesha joked about Snacks being in the bathroom for that long.

"I'm telling you y'all better have bus fare. Y'all tryin real hard to get left" he threatened while he cut into his steak. After dropping the girls off Snacks called both Beef and Reese and informed them that he had something real important to talk about. *Phase one operation clean up is about to be in effect* he thought as he rode to the sounds of *Meek Mills Dreamchasers 2.*

# CHAPTER 18

S NACKS DECIDED THAT they should meet at a neutral spot so that Both Reese and Beef would feel comfortable. He chose Branch Brook Park by the skating rink. Snacks was the first to arrive followed by Beef. When Beef arrived, Snacks was leaning against his car talking to Reema on the phone. Beef stepped out of his car and greeted his brother "As-Salamu-Alaykum."

"Walaykum Salaam" Snacks greeted him back as he hung up with Reema.

"What's so important" Beef questioned.

"I got something big on the table for us but ima wait till Reese get here to-.

"Beef cut him off "I already told you I'm not fuckin wit ya man like that" Beef said sternly. Snacks looked at his brother directly in his eyes so he could see the seriousness within them.

"This shit I got lined up is bigger that lil bullshit beef yall got going on. We gonna get rich. Now if yall can't squash yall lil situation for this paper then yall ain't the niggas I thought yall was." Beef looked away. "Look at me "Beef was still being stubborn." Bra I said look at me!!! "Snacks demanded." "I got Pedro Martinez backin me." Hearing Pedro's name got Beef's attention immediately.

"You stylin "Beef said not believing his brother had a plug of Pedro's magnitude.

"Nigga what I got to lie—

Before Snacks could finish his statement Reese pulled up. He got out the he and Snacks hugged tightly. By both of them doing time it separated them for just about 12 years. "I love you but I can't fuck with your brotha." Reese said as the two embraced.

"Listen bra, we got some major shit on da line and I need yall to get on the same page."

Knowing Snacks would never put him in harm's way Reese heard him out. He was hesitant at first but after Snacks gave him the same spiel he gave his brother Reese was in, and they all left the park on the same page and on the same mission. It was time to fulfil his promise to Rik and take what was his. "The streets are mine" Snacks said as he rode by himself leaving the meeting.

## Later That Night

Rah was eager to prove to Snacks he was really on his side. So he stalked P's baby mother's house like a predator. After sitting outside her house until the wee hours of the morning. P finally pulled up at about 4:30 Am. Before P's feet could touch the pavement, Rah boxed in unloading his 17 shot P90. When it was all said and done, 10 shots hit P. two in the head, two the neck and the rest in his chest and stomach.

## *Later That Morning*

Snacks woke up to a text from Rah telling him to go to RLS Media. Snacks didn't have to read the article because Amanda sat in front of the TV watching channel 12, the New Jersey news channel. The reporter was reporting a murder that took place just a few hours earlier. When P's picture had flashed across the screen, Snacks knew Rah had done his assignment and the reporter said they had no leads. Snacks looked at Rah in a new light. "Maybe he gonna work out after all" Snacks said a little louder than he attended to.

"You said something baby?" Amanda said looking back at him.

"Nah everything cool babe."

"Well let me make sure" she said while pushing him back down and burying her face in his lap.

"Damn I think I'm in love" he said looking at her go to work.

Snacks was really starting to love her but after talking to Reema, he realized how much he missed his family. He just couldn't put his issues with her behind him because she was still lying about getting him sent back to prison. He told her that they could just work on their relationship if she just tell the truth. Yet, she still denied getting him sent back. Not to mention shit was about to get crazy and she still was fucking with Nikki. After that day in the store as far as he was concerned she was the enemy too!

## 45 MINUTES LATER

Snacks got dressed and rode through North 5th, he was looking for a young boy he had been in the County with. The young boy always bragged about him and his crew always having stolen cars on deck in case they had to put in work. Snacks had a car Asap! He wanted to get operation cleanup done and over with. He planned on hitting both Swift and Sheed today. Snacks hoped the young boy wasn't just talking because now was the time to show and prove. He spotted a group of young boys standing in front of the town houses. He stopped and rolled the window down. One of the boys stepped forward

"Wats Crackin Homeboy!"

"Sav out here?" Snacks yelled.

"Who askin?" the boy said.

"Hold up, let me pull over. Snacks pulled out the middle of the street to the curb and got out. Sav spotted him from wherever he was and came running.

"Big bra, what's good?" he was excited to see Snacks.

"What's good wit you bra?" Snacks said shaking his hand, pulling him in for a light hug.

"You already know I'm out here chasin' this paper." Sav admitted.

"That's cool, I don't know what ya situation is but ima have something real nice inna coupla weeks" Snacks informed him.

"You know ima fuck wit you big bra."

"Say no more but right now I need a G-ride."

"What you lookin for?" Sav asked him like he owned a car lot.

"It really don't matter as long as it's fast and it's not already hot."

"I would never play you like that, I got the perfect thing for you." Sav said leading the way down the street. As they walked, they laughed and joked about the time they spent in the County. "Here she go right here" Sav stopped in front of an All-Black 2014 Audi A8.

"Yeah this what I'm talking about, this will definitely do" Snacks said showing his approval. "How much you want for this baby?" Snacks asked digging in his pockets. Sav stopped him.

"Don't insult me, you good, we family."

"You sure?" Snacks asked double checking.

"Stop playing, I said you good."

"Ok cool A'ight bet. Ima send my lil man to come pick it up later."

"Here take my number, hit me before you send him through so I could make sure everything good." With that, they shook hands and parted ways.

## Later That Night

Snacks sat behind the wheel of the Audi waiting on Swift, Sheed or Rik to come out of Riverview. Just so happen, Swift had just set up some pussy with a local hood rat named Becky. Becky wasn't bad looking she just had a lot of dick on her jacket. It was also a rumor that Becky had H.I.V but as time went on the rumor proved to be false. The rumor was started by a kid named Weedy, Weedy had a thing for Becky. After Becky sexed him real good one night he wanted more than just a one night stand but the whore in her wouldn't let her commit to a relationship and Weedy couldn't understand that. Once everybody found out it was him that started the rumor nobody took it serious.

With Becky having the reputation like she did, Swift didn't want nobody to see her getting in his car. So he made plans to meet her at the bar in Hyatt Court. Swift pulled out of Riverview with one thing on his mind...Pussy! So he wasn't on point when the Audi pulled off from the top of the projects behind him. Swift made it pass the first light but got stuck at the second one. When his vehicle came to a complete stop, Snacks sped up and cut in front of him. Just as he went to curse out the driver of the Audi, the passenger and rear doors popped open. Reese and Beef sprayed Swift's car with Assault rifles, they left his car smoking and Swift lifeless.

## LATER THAT SAME NIGHT

At the hospital Rik consoled Swift's mother and girlfriend, promising them he wasn't going to let his friend's death go unanswered for. But the truth was he was scared shitless. He knew Snacks was behind the murders of P and Swift but it was like he was fighting a ghost. Snacks was yet to be seen but he was making his presence felt.

Rik and Sheed sat in the parking lot of Rutgers AKA U.M.D Hospital in panic mode. "What the fuck is happening?" Rik yelled in frustration.

"Oh you don't know what's going on?" Sheed asked sarcastically.

"Now ain't the time my nigga, Now ain't the time" Rik said sternly.

"I don't know what you 'bout to do but ima slide down the 'A' for a while" Sheed said.

"So you running now?" Rik questioned tryna play on his manhood.

"Look my nigga I don't care what you say! That nigga ain't gon stop till we kill him or he kill YOU!" Sheed put emphasis on the word you.

"You know what? Get out my car" Rik mushed Sheed and before he knew it they were out the car fighting and Nikki was dragging them apart. When they were finally separated, Nikki was in his ear screaming

"What's gotten into you? Swift just lost his life and out here acting crazy."

"Nik I'm not tryna hear that shit right now" Rik said walking off.

"Where are you going?" "I'ma take your car, take mine and I'll see you later" he said as he walked toward her car. Seconds later he pulled out of the hospital parking lot.

"That's his bitch right there! We should smoke her for the fun of it" Beef said from the back seat as they watched Nikki's car pull out the parking lot.

"Easy big bra, I've been waiting on this moment for years now. I'm not fuckin this up for nobody" Snacks said from the passenger seat. Snacks and Reese had switched spots and it was his turn to put in work. "Here he come now." Snacks brought everybody's attention to Rik's Range Rover pulling out the parking lot.

They watched as Rik's Range Rover turned right on Bergen St. and headed towards West Market St. As soon as the Range Rover made it past Checkers, Reese sped up and dipped around her when he made it in front of her he hit his breaks causing her to stop short. *Beeeeep* she hit the horn of the Range "Muthafucka" Just as the words left her mouth the passenger door of the Audi swung open. Snacks stepped out and let the Choppa rip like he was Rambo. The first 2 shots ripped through the windshield smashing into Nikki's chest, then a bullet pierced her face. Bullets riddled her body, she was dead long before Snacks had finished shooting. Snacks didn't know it was Nikki driving because the front windshield of the Range was limo tinted. As far as he knew he thought he had fulfilled his promise to Rik by killing him.

# CHAPTER 19

S NACKS PHONE WOULDN'T allow him to sleep. Someone
was calling him nonstop. He was mad enough to throw it against
the wall and break it. "What!" he answered without looking at
the caller I.D. Reema was hysterical on the other end.

"You fuckin monster! "How could you?"

"What the fuck are you talkin about?" he played dumb.

"You stupid bastard! That was Nikki in Rink's tru----"

He cut her off. "I don't know what you're talkin about" he continued
his act.

"I bet you do. That was Nikki in Rik's truck last night" she repeated.
"And to make matters worse, Lil Rik was in the backseat Snacks. They
said he might not walk again. He's just a fuckin baby you monster. Stay
away from me and my daughter! Karma is a bitch and when she knock
on your door I'm not going to be around." Reema didn't give him a

chance to reply she just hung up on him, leaving him stunned. He could give a shit about Nikki but damn Lil Rik was only 7 years old.

"Fuck it! Nobody didn't give a fuck when he had my cousin killed. I told that nigga I would kill his whole family If I had to. When are people gonna learn that when I say something I mean it! Fuck it! I mine as well get up" he said after failing to go back to sleep after several attempts.

Amanda had once again left the TV on the New Jersey News channel before going to work. As Snacks dried his wet body from the shower he had just taken. He watched the reporter describe the murder of a young woman and the shooting of her young son as animalistic. Snacks had no sorrow he just wished Rik was in the car too. Now he would have to start hunting again today. It didn't matter how long it took, he was determined to kill Rik and everybody who stood in his way. "I need another whip" he said while dialing Sav's number.

"Yo what up bra?"

"Ain't shit just another day another dollar" Sav said cooly.

"I hear you lil bra, you think you could come through for me again?" Snacks questioned.

"I told you I stay wit something" Sav bragged.

"Ok cool, same routine as last time."

"Aight say no more" Sav confirmed. "Oh and Big bra."

"What up nigga?" Snacks questioned.

"I see ya work my boy" Sav said letting Snacks know he'd seen the news.

"You know the shit" Snacks laughed and hung up.

### An Hour Later

After getting dressed and making it to Newark. Snacks sat in front of Beef's house waiting for him to come out. Beef finally came out 15 minutes later. "Damn bra! You take longer than a woman to get dressed" Snacks joked as Beef slammed the door to the Lincoln.

"I rather you wait on me than me wait on your slow ass" Beef replied. "Yo I know you seen the news" Beef mentioned while turning the radio down.

"Yeah shit crazy" Snacks admitted.

"It's only one or two things that'll come out of this."

"And what's that?" Snacks asked curiously.

"Either he gonna go hard or he gonna tuck his tail and hide."

"Well I prefer he don't hide" Snacks said coming to a stop at a light on Elizabeth Ave and Meeka. "I got a plan anyway" Snacks said rubbing his bearded chin.

"And what's that?"

"We'll wait until the obituary comes out, find out where the burial gonna be and catch him there." Beef looked at his brother like he was crazy.

"You can't be serious."

"Im dead ass serious" Snacks said before getting on Route 22 to go see Ashlee.

## 15 Minutes Later

Snacks was sitting in Ashlee's 2008 Honda Accord getting to know her a little. He found out that Apple Bees was her second job. Her first job was being a home health aide. Through his inquires he found out she had no kids, she lived alone and liked to have fun as she put it. From his experiences with women he knew when they said they just liked to have fun meant they liked to fuck so Snacks knew he had a freak. While Snacks was in the car with Ashlee, Rah called and let him know he picked the car up from Sav.

## Later That Night

Snacks got up with Ashlee and just like she said, she like to have fun. That's exactly what they did...Have fun. Snacks smashed her all through her house. In all types of positions, she took it in every hole.

Ashlee was a wild girl. Snacks still made it home to Amanda by 12:30 Am. She was sound asleep when he got in, he took a shower and slid in the bed next to her like it was nothing.

### 5 Days Later

Rose Hill Cemetery in Linden New Jersey was packed. People from all walks of life came out to show their last respects to Nikki. Her son wasn't able to attend the funeral because he was still in a coma. Rik sat in a wooden fold up chair in his black Armani suit and his Saint Laurent shades with his head hung low, weeping uncontrollably. He loved Nikki and words couldn't explain his hurt. Rik stayed at the grave site long after everybody left. He blamed himself because he knew with Snacks hot in pursuit of him, he should have never let her drive his car. "Ima ride on that nigga bae. I promise that nigga is gonna die!!!" he stood up. As soon as he stood up, Snacks stepped out the F-150 pickup with a choppa in his hand. Rik looked up just in time. Snacks fired the choppa like he was trained by the U.S Army. Rik dove behind a big oak tree. Snacks closed in on him rapidly. He fired a few more shots while closing in on Rik. Snacks was surprised when Rik returned fire with his 17 shot Gllock 40. This caused Snacks to slow down and duck behind a tree himself. Rik used this as his chance to make it to his BMW 750. Just as he made it to his car, Snacks fired again. This time striking Rik in his leg. Rik had his mind set, he wasn't dying. He had a son to live for. Rik made it back to his car as Snacks made it back to the F150.

"Don't let that nigga get away" Snacks said hopping in the truck out of breath.

"Which way?" Reese questioned.

"Go over the grass."

"Over the grass?" both Beef and Reese asked at the same time.

"Yeah over the grass."

"Bra don't go over no grass" Beef said stopping Reese from carrying out Snacks' order. "We need to get outta here with less attention as possible and this ain't no movie." Beef said.

"Fuck!!!" Snacks said slapping the dashboard.

"Calm down we gon catch em" Beef reasoned.

"It's like this pussy got 9 lives" Snacks said mad he missed his target.

As Rik came speeding out the cemetery recklessly, Linden police were coming down Route 1&9 to respond to heard gunshots. They jumped on him immediately. He continued to take the chase down 1&9 reaching speeds as high as 150 Mph. Rik was near the Budweiser Factory in Newark with Linden and Elizabeth police behind him. When he couldn't handle the speed of the chase anymore he crashed into another car, before hitting the divider, Rik flipped 3 times in the BMW which resulted in 4 broken ribs, a broken nose and dislocated shoulder. Rik was lucky to survive, he escaped Snacks again now he has to answer to the law for the gun in the car and the eluting. Not to mention the injured people in the car he hit. Rik was still alive but he was in deep shit. On top of all that, Newark homicide detectives wanted to talk to him about who might have wanted him dead enough to kill his wife and shoot his 7 year old son.

# CHAPTER 20

REEMA FELT LIKE her life was falling apart. Her marriage was just about over and her best friend was dead. Reema sat in Nikki's storage cleaning it out. This was a spot only her and Nikki knew about. This was Nikki's stash spot where she kept money that she'd stolen from Rik. She also kept pictures, diaries, old cds and gifts she had gotten from other guys she had dated when Rik acted up. Reema sat on a crate and looked at an old photo album. The memories brought tears to her eyes. Reema was hurt Snacks could carry out such a vicious act. Reema put the photo album down and picked up a diary that had been laying on top of a box. She picked it up and flipped to one of the last entrees Nikki had written.

As Reema read what Nikki wrote she was crushed her best friend would cross her like the way she did. Reading Nikki's diary, Reema learned that Nikki was the cause of the troubles that plagued her marriage. Reema was hot, she wished she could confront her but Nikki was dead and Reema was alone.

Highly upset, Reema decided to leave Nikki's stuff where it was. She couldn't believe all this time her best friend was a snake. Reema was loyal to Nikki even against Snacks' wishes. Just like he said "It would come back and bite you in the ass." She had to call him and apologize. She hate to admit it but he was right all along. "I got to try and call him, I hope he picks up" she wished. With no luck, Snacks sent her call straight to voicemail so she sent him a text.

Snacks sat at the table eating dinner at Pedro's house with Amanda. He was enjoying himself when he got a call from Reema followed by a text. Upon receiving the call and text his whole mood changed in a blink of an eye. Amanda picked up on his mood swing immediately.

"Baby is everything OK?" She asked genuinely.

"Everything cool." He replied casually. "Now like I was saying." Snacks continued. "I'm ready whenever you are." He looked directly at Pedro as he spoke.

"Daddy I'm going to the kitchen" Amanda said excusing herself from the table. Snacks loved that she never stuck around when he talked business. She really knew her place and Snacks appreciated her for it. When Amanda was out of earshot, Pedro spoke just above a whisper.

"I've been watching the news and I see you've been working hard" Snacks listened attentively as Pedro praised him. "It's not the fact that you were able to eliminate your enemies that I like. You know what I like?" Pedro questioned.

"And what might that be?" Snacks asked.

"I like that you did it without making yourself hot. That's the good part."

"Well thank you sir" Snacks said modestly.

"The fact you are not hot lets me know you're good at what you do" Pedro continued to praise Snacks. "Now let's get down to business" Pedro said clapping his hands once. "I'm going to give you Birds of pure heroin at 50 thousand a key. How does that sound?" Pedro questioned Snacks.

"That's great. That gives me enough room to do whatever I need to" Snacks said knowing 50 bands for pure dope was a come up.

"Well this is what we'll do" Pedro paused for a moment. "I'm going to give you 2 keys. One you can give me 50 thousand for and the other one you can give me 25 thousand for. This is so you can get your money up. I never expect you to come short and all losses comes out of your pocket... Understand?" Pedro spoke sternly.

"Yes sir I understand" Snacks said never looking away while speaking to Pedro. He wanted him to know he meant business just like he did.

"I have a man who has a master mix that will guarantee you will always have the best product on the street. Using this mix you can turn one key into two and it will still be an 8 or 9."

"I like the way that sounds" Snacks admitted.

"But like everything in life, it cost and he only sells it by thee key" Pedro said.

"Ok cool, get me a key" Snacks said shaking Pedro's hand to seal the deal. "Thank you sir, you've been to kind to me. I promise you won't be sorry."

"Son, I have very little doubt you will do anything other than make me proud" Pedro said patting him on the back.

### The Next Day

One of Pedro's men dropped off a 2014 Honda Odyssey Van equipped with a stash box with the 2 keys of dope and the key of cut in it. Now All Snacks had to do was assemble a team to work the table with him. He started with two fiends that had watched him grow up in the game he would also use these two in his building to sale the dope once he set up shop. Jeff and Mike were very trustworthy. Even though they got high all the time, they proved to be trustworthy. They would be in charge of stamping all the empty dope bags.

Next he reached out and asked Ashlee if she would be down to work the table. She said she's down and she has a sister who needs extra money so he could count Carmen in as well. Lastly he placed a call to one of favorite cousins on his father's side. Snacks really didn't fuck with his father's side of the family like that, but him and Lisa where like brother and sister. The bond they shared was special, they would do anything for one another so without her needing much detail, and she was in. Snacks wanted to get started early so he told everybody to be ready by 9am. He dropped the boxes of empty dope bags and stamps off to Jeff and Mike so by the morning all they would have to do was cut the dope and put in the bags. Snacks also took the time to show each member how to fold and tape each bag. Reese had a spot down Hyatt where they would put everything together.

With everything set up for the morning Snacks decided to stop by Reema's house before heading home. When Snacks rang the doorbell he was greeted by Neesha standing in the doorway with her hand on her hip. "I hope you're here to stay." She said with a little more attitude than Snacks liked.

"First of all take your hand off your hip when you're talkin to me, second stop talkin to me like you gave birth to me." Snacks checked her. Reema stood at a short distance watching the exchange.

"That's what I've been going through since you haven't been here." Reema informed him. "She think she grown." Reema added.

"You better tone it down." Snacks demanded looking at his daughter. He hated being hard on Neesha but he refused to have a fast ass little girl. "You hear me?" Snacks questioned taking off his jacket sitting on the couch.

"Yes daddy, I hear you I'm sorry, it's just that I'm not used to you being home and not being here with us. "As she spoke Neesh's head hung low and her face was sad. Seeing his baby like this made Snacks feel bad.

"I'm sorry baby." He apologized. "Don't worry about me and your mother we'll be fine, we just need to work a few things out."

"Ok daddy" She said with a hint of a smile.

"Come give me a hug" He said standing up. As they hugged he kissed her forehead. "Now get out of here and let grown people talk."

"I love you daddy"

"I Love you too" He confirmed as she headed up stairs.

Reema and Snacks talked for about 2 hours. She told Snacks about the diary she found in Nikki's storage. She also apologized for not listening to him about Nikki being a snake. She admitted she was sorry for not fighting for their marriage as hard as she should have. Snacks agreed that they could start repairing their marriage slowly. He told her he would always remain loyal to Amanda because she was there for him when he had one else. It was hard pill to swallow, but she did because she understood that Amanda only existed in their lives because she allowed her to slide in when she slipped. So for now she would put up with her and that was only for now.

Reema tried to have sex with him but Snacks declined he told her it was too soon. He was still being stubborn. Reema felt like she was the side chick. She wanted her man back so for now she would let him have his cake and eat it too, The fact that she knew once he left he would be going home to another female made her sick to her stomach. This whole shit is Nikki's fault she thought as she went to the bathroom to run herself a hot bath. "I wish that bitch was alive so I could kill her my dam self." Reema said while slipping into the warm water filled with bubbles. Reema cried while she soaked she was truly sick.

Amanda was still up when Snacks got in. The whole ride home he was trying to find a way to tell Amanda he was going to be staying back at Reema's again. When he walked in the bedroom Amanda had scented candles lit, soft music playing and she was laid in the middle of the bed looking stunning. "What's all this?" He asked while waving his hand around the room.

"Well, I thought we would celebrate." She said gingerly.

"Celebrate what?"

"This." She said pulling a home pregnancy test from behind her back. He was speechless. Snacks took a little too long to respond and Amanda took it wrong. She started crying hysterically. He tried to hug her but she snatched away. 'Don't touch me, you don't want my baby." She accused.

"What!!! Are you crazy? Why would you say somethin like that?" At this point Snacks had raised his voice matching Amanda's energy.

"Because you didn't say anything." Amanda continued to sob.

"Because I'm speechless that's why. I didn't think you would want to bring a child into this world with me. I'm just a criminal -----

"Amanda cut him off before he could finish downing himself. "Who I am madly in love with." She looked at his face for confirmation.

"I love you too baby" He confirmed before she continued.

"And in case you haven't noticed Pedro Martinez is my father."

"I'm aware that I'm about to have a baby with the mafia princess." He joked. This brought a smile to Amanda's face.

"So you're happy about the baby?"

"Of course I am." He said kissing her flat stomach. She searched his eyes for the true and at that moment she knew he would be in her life forever.

# CHAPTER 21

EARLY THE NEXT morning. Snacks sat with the rest of the team cutting and bagging the dope. Even though Pedro told him that each kilo could be turned into two Snacks decided he would make his dope stronger using less cut. So, what he did was he put 400 grams of the potent mix from Pedro's people on each kilo which gave him an extra 800 grams. When it was all said and done Snacks had 2600 bricks. He would put 2000 bricks in the building, getting $200 a brick and he would wholesale the remaining 600 of them. After he paid Pedro back his $75,000 he will still profit at least 250 stacks and that's after shorts and losses.

He wouldn't have a problem selling the dope because it was fire. After he mixed it down before bagging it up he gave Mike some to sniff and Jeff some to shoot. Snacks laughed so hard tears came out his eyes when he went back in the living room to ask how the dope was. They both were in a nod so deep it looked like they were sleep. As Snacks entered the living room he already knew the answer to his question.

His next step would be which building he would use in Riverview to set up shop. It was simple to him that building 3 would be his choice. Building 3 was prime real estate. In this building you had a fiend on each floor so he planned to pay each one of them to keep their door unlocked for whoever working in the building.

After establishing his spot, it was time to put his product out. Snacks passed out samples his whole first day out. The next day Reese would set up shop early in the morning with Jeff. Jeff would play the building while Reese directed traffic. Reese's shift would be from 5 A.M. until 3 P.M. then Snacks would take over with Mike from 3.PM. until 11P.M. Rah would have the night shift, that way someone would always be in the building working. Beef would go back on 11ᵗʰ street and run his spot however he saw fit.

Even though all the dope was the same, Snacks made two different names. Takeover and Blueprint. He did this because he knew how fiends were. One would say they like takeover better than blueprint and vice versa and it would be the same thing. They would swear it wasn't, once a fiend was stuck on a certain name that's what they wanted.

The first day they opened shop they sold 75 bricks. At 200 a brick that was 15 stacks, not bad for their first day. Snacks had bigger dreams, if they could do 75 bricks on each shift that would be great. With that in mind he pushed his team harder and harder each day. By end of the week they sold 750 bricks. He had paid Pedro and was waiting on his next 2 keys.

## WEEKS LATER

Snacks had finally finished his first shipment. After shorts, paying the workers and paying the people in the building, the 3 of them split $350,000. Not bad for 3 ½ weeks of work. Snacks' first month back, he already had 100 stacks and that was only with Riverview court and South 11ᵗʰ St. He couldn't wait to expand, the way the hood responded to takeover and blueprint, Snacks was sure that he was about to put the city in a headlock.

Snacks even reached out to Sav and gave him 50 bricks he told him to put it in his hood to see what it do. Sav let Snacks know that all he sold was coke and his block was a coke block only do he doubted he would make any real noise but to his surprise once he gave out samples, Dope fiends flooded his block Lke Katrina. Snacks told Sav he could keep the 50 bricks for looking out for him with the cars. Sav couldn't wait for the next shipment because his block wanted that takeover bad.

## A Little Over 3 Months Later

Things were going great, Snacks was seeing more money than he had in his whole life. The hood was running smooth, 11<sup>th</sup> street was doing numbers, Sav was doing 100 bricks a week and Shock had come home and jumped right on board. Newarky came home but he wasn't fucking around in the dope game. He was stuck on some web series that he was writing but he did plug Snacks in with Rocky and Qua out Elizabeth in a projects called Bayway. Newarky warned Snacks not to fuck with Qua because Qua was slimy but Snacks fucked with him anyway. Snacks reasoned that Qua couldn't be no Slimier than the dudes in Newark that he dealt with already. Little did Snacks know, Qua took slimy to a whole new level. Rocky on the other hand was a good business dude. He paid on time, he was never short and sometimes he paid for his work up front. Business was good for the most part. Snacks had spots in Newark, Elizabeth and in Carteret. Snacks no longer let Pedro front him 2 keys at a time, he was now paying for 5 keys up front. He would turn the 5 keys he bought into 8 keys using the mix he had gotten from Pedro's people. 8 keys would make him 6,000 brick and his goal was to move all 6,000 bricks in 1 month or less.

Pedro loved Snacks and he kept him on point. Pedro told Snacks he didn't have to sell bricks, he could sell keys but Snacks was in love with the streets. Pedro told Snacks he would put him so high on the food chain he would never even have to be seen. Snacks respectfully declined his offer.

Snacks wanted to make it to the top but not because Pedro put him there, he wanted to earn it. Snacks knew Pedro was trying to help him out because of the baby. Snacks wanted his way, on his terms! Even though Snacks was making a large amount of cash, he still stayed low. He knew he dodged a bullet with the law one time already with Rik, so he didn't want to keep pressing his luck. Rik had kept it gangsta when the police questioned him he told them he didn't know who shot him or who shot his son and killed his wife. Rik was a lot of things but a snitch he wasn't, he chose to keep it in the streets and Snacks respected him for that if nothing else.

Rik never bailed out after the accident. He stayed in Union County Jail on the medical pod. He used his time to heal and get his mind right. His son had come out of the coma and had to learn how to walk all over again. Thinking of his son's struggles drove him almost insane not to mention the time he was facing. Rik was offered a 5 with a 5 meaning the state wanted him to do 5 years. He didn't want to do 5 years but he needed the time to get right both mentally and physically. When he finally did get right, Snacks will die. He now using the beef between him and Snacks as motivation. Snacks had come home, in a short period of time he killed some of the closest people to him and managed to take the projects back. Rik's thought only added to his hate "What goes up must come down and when you come down I'll be right here waiting" Rik said to no one particular.

# CHAPTER 22

B EEF RODE THROUGH Riverview at a slow pace. He watched the flow from behind the tinted windows of his new 2014 Chrysler 300m SRT8. Since they landed their new plug, they'd been benefitting financially. He had to admit Snacks and Reese had things running like clockwork. Beef stopped in front of building 3 and hit the horn twice, Reese looked out the window. Beef rolled the passenger window down. "You busy?" Beef asked over the music coming from his radio.

"Not really, I'm coming down" moments later Reese exited the building getting in the car.

"What up?" Beef spoke as they shook hands.

"Ain't shit, about to shut down for a few. Hawaii rollin hard!" Hawaii was a code they use for police.

"A'ight cool let's shoot out to Elizabeth to see if we could catch the nigga Qua" Beef said pulling out the projects.

This was really the first time Beef and Reese rode together without Snacks. As Beef sped up Route 1&9 towards Elizabeth. Beef turned down the radio and spoke

"Bra I just wanted to say I respect your gangsta. I never knew it was you we was tryna get" Beef admitted. "And I apolo-" Reese cut him off.

"No need my nigga. We past that. I realize you didn't know who I was at first. I hadn't been thinkin like that when shit first kicked off. We had already both lost homies and I got hit. I was mad but I know if we knew each other that would have never went down. We good my nigga" Reese said shaking Beef's hand once again.

## 20 Minutes Later

They walked through Bayway looking for Qua. The niggas in projects looked at the two strangers and knew they came for trouble. Rocky spotted them from one of the buildings and called them over.

"What brings yall out this way?" Rocky asked shaking hands with them both.

"Where ya man Qua at?" Beef asked watching Rocky closely.

"I knew that nigga did some bullshit" Rocky said. "You see that hallway over there. He over there playin dice" Rocky pointed out.

"Good lookin my nigga" Reese said as they walked away headed to the hallway. The guys in the hallway were caught off guard when Beef and Reese slid in.

"What's poppin?" Beef yelled being the first one in the hallway. Qua looked up and knew they came to put work in. one of the guys that was playing in the dice game tried to draw his weapon but Reese shot him sending him to the ground. Once he hit the floor, Reese was on him immediately taking his gun. "What's up wit dat bread?" Beef asked standing over Qua.

"I'mma get I..I..I.." Qua stuttered.

"Wrong answer" Beef smacked Qua across the bridge of his nose with his gun, breaking his nose.

"AHH shit" Qua screamed, grabbing his face as blood squirted everywhere, painting the walls red.

Beef continued to pistol-whip Qua until he was out cold. When he was knocked out, Reese went in his pockets, relieving him of the money he had on him. Before leaving out the hall, Reese kicked Qua in the face, waking him up. "Next time we come through here, you betta have dat bread," Reese threatened as they left.

Snacks had started spending more time at Reema's house. They weren't how they were before, but they were trying and she was happy to have him around. He had even upgraded her Cherokee to a 2014. They had started having sex occasionally. Reema was sure that in due time snacks would be all her's again. On the other hand, his relationship with Amanda seemed to grow more and more each day. Things were getting hard for him because juggling two women was easy when your heart was attached to both of them. He still hadn't told Reema that Amanda was pregnant. Things were so much easier when him and Reema were beefing. Amanda being pregnant gave a certain type of glow.

The bigger she got, the more she shined. Snacks had grown to love her. She was the perfect woman. He didn't have to hide the fact that he had been spending time with his family. He just did it respectfully. Amanda knew Snacks loved her so the time he spent with Reema didn't matter to her. She understood what she was getting into when she allowed herself to love him, so Amanda was secure in her spot. Her and snacks had an unbreakable bond. She understood him and he understood her and that was all that mattered.

# CHAPTER 23

SNACKS AND AMANDA walked through The Garden State Plaza Mall hand and hand. They were shopping for the baby, the two looked happy as newlyweds. "Baby my feet are starting to hurt. Let's stop in Johnny Rocket's and get something to eat."

"I don't see why your feet are hurtin it's not like you carrin no bags." Snacks joked. His joke earned him a punch in the arm from Amanda. "Ouch" Snacks rubbed his arm faking pain. "You know it's whatever you want. I got you." Snacks was happy to comply with Amanda's wishes. He loved making her happy. She treated him like a king, so she deserved to be treated like nothing less than royalty herself.

"That's why I love you." She admitted.

"And why is that?"

"Because you always got me." She said stopping to kiss him. They kissed briefly before entering the restaurant. They choose to sit in a cozy both in the corner. When they were seated and settled Amanda slid her feet out of her Dior flats and placed in Snacks lap. He massaged her feet under the table. "Damn that feels so good" She said closing her eyes enjoying every moment.

"You know you owe me for this right?" He teased.

"Yes!!! Anything you want" She agreed sounding like she was on the verge of having an orgasm.

"Anything?" He questioned.

"Yes, anything baby."

"You know what I want." He smirked devilishly.

"You so nasty. Why does the night always have to end with my mouth on your penis?"

"It's just you're so good at what you do." He laughed.

"You think you're so funny" She said throwing a bald up napkin at him.

The napkin missed him and landed on the floor. He bent down to pick up the napkin. When he got back up Reema and Neesha was standing behind Amanda, Reema to say Reema looked hurt would have been an understatement. Reema had tears in her eyes and everything.

"So you playin house wit this bitch?" She spit her words with venom while pointing at Amanda's stomach.

"Don't start." He warned.

"Don't start, don't start!!! Nigga you got this bitch pregnant?"

"Who you callin a bitch??" Amanda tried to get up but Snacks stopped her.

"Don't" He looked at her. She returned his stare with fury in her eyes, but obeyed him. "You better get your-----" She started to match Reema's level of disrespect but she stopped herself. For 1 Neesha was present, and 2 that wasn't her style. She respected Snacks too much to get disrespectful in front of his daughter, even if her mother was acting like a bitch.

"Thank you" Snacks said rubbing Amanda's shoulder.

"Don't thank that bitch. Let her get and get her ass beat." Reema was putting on a show and she didn't care who was watching. "Reema I'm not going to tell again." Snacks spoke in a low tone that still let her know not to fuck with him. He was really trying to control hus anger.

"Oh, so you gon put your hands on me for this bitch? Nigga you got da game fucked up" Snacks attempted to walk up on her. Reema snatched Neesha's soda and threw it in Snack's face. Soda splashed all over. He was pissed. He lunged at her grabbing her by her collar. He was about to raise his hand when Neesha spoke up.

"Daddy please don't." His baby girl pleaded.

"You lucky" He said while letting Reema loose and taking a step back.

"Yeah nigga you betta had" She said still talking shit.

"Ma why don't you just stop." Neesha begged.

"Come on we out." Reema said pulling Neesha by the arm. Neesha pulled away from her mother gently.

"I'ma stay wit my father." This not only shocked Reema but it only made her madder than she already was.

"You know what, you stay wit your no good as father. See if he still have time for her time for you when that bitch have that lil bastard she carrying" Again Amanda tried to get up and again Snacks stopped her. Amanda was sick of Reema's disrespect.

"I'm sorry "Snacks apologized for Reema's ill behavior.

"It's not your fault" Amanda said while Neesha just sat down looking sad.

"I know I have a lot of explaining to do and I promise I will but let me get a shirt out of one of these stores and we could talk" he promised Neesha as he got up from the table. "You want to come with me?" he asked his daughter.

"No I'm good daddy Ima sit here with your girlfriend."

"Well for starters her name is Amanda and you be nice."

"Daddy I have manners" Neesha replied.

"You better" he said before stepping off.

When Snacks was gone it was an awkward silence at first. Then Amanda broke the ice.

"I've heard so much about you" Amanda said.

"I wish I could say the same" Neesha said truthfully.

"I told your dad to wait to tell you until the time was right" Amanda admitted.

"Why?" Neesha questioned.

"Because I know you're used to being the only one and I didn't want you to feel like we..." Amanda said rubbing her stomach "...Were trying to take your place."

"Is it true what my mom said about my dad not having time for me when you have your baby?"

"First of all, this is all of our baby. We are all family now. Your father has a big heart. You're his princess and that will never change." Hearing Amanda say that drew a smile on Neesha's face.

"Do you know what you're having?" Neesha questioned.

"We're having a boy."

"A boy, so Ima have a little brother?" Neesha asked excitedly.

"Yup, you sure are."

"Can I touch your stomach?" Neesha asked.

"Sure come on this side" Amanda said sliding over for Neesha to sit next to her. Neesha slid next to her and put her hand on Amanda's stomach, rubbing it lightly. As she was rubbing Amanda's stomach, she felt the baby kick.

"You felt that?" Neesha asked amazed.

"Oh god yes" Amanda laughed causing Neesha to as well. As the two were laughing Snacks walked up.

"Ok it's good to see yall getting along" he said taking a seat.

"Daddy I'm mad at you."

"Why princess?"

"Because I wanted to be mad at you for having another girlfriend but Amanda is mad cool."

"Aw thanks Neesha" Amanda said hugging her. They finished their meal and went home. Snacks slept in the living room while Neesha slept in bed with Amanda.

The situation with Snacks was becoming too much for Reema to handle. She was crushed. She knew he had another woman but to see him with her own eyes all hugged up was something she wasn't prepared for. To top it all off that bitch had the nerve to be pregnant. Reema was starting to hate Snacks. For the last few days Reema found herself depressed. She had no one to share her problems with. Even though

Nikki was the root of her troubles she wished Nikki was alive to be her crutch at a time when it seemed like she couldn't stand up and fight. Reema was tiered sitting around sulking. Tonight she was going out and she was going to have FUN.

Hours later Reema sat in a bar out in Elizabeth called Terminal One with the tightest dress you've ever seen. At first sight you tell she definitely came out to have FUN, as Snacks called it. She was sitting at the bar totally wasted, but she kept going. Reema turned around as she felt someone in back of her. "Let me get two of whatever she's having" The man said as he pointed to Reema. He had been watching her sit at the bar getting fucked up and figured now would be a good time to make his move. "What's up sexy?" He asked. "My name is Qua" he introduced himself as he stuck his hand out for a handshake. Reema looked at his hand like it had shit on it. Qua wasn't really her type, he was light-skin, Kind of on the scrawny side and had a big head but she had to admit she like the way he dressed. He looked kind of fly in his all-black Gucci sweat suit with the red and green stripe going across the chest.

"Wassup with you?" Reema said drunkenly.

"You want another?" He said sliding one of the shots the bartender came back with in front of her.

"I don't think I should" she said while hiccupping.

"One more ain't gonna hurt" he persuaded.

"Ok just one" She gave in.

10 shots and an hour later she had agreed to let him drive her home in her car. First she said no but Qua told her no real man would ever let her drive home in the condition she was in. Once again she let him game her into doing what he wanted her to do. Usually Reema was smarter than what she was tonight but at the moment she was so mad at Snacks she didn't give a fuck.

Once they made it to her truck, Qua helped her get in. He took full advantage of her by feeling all over her. She didn't stop him because she knew she wouldn't let it get any further than that. After helping her in, Qua jumped in the driver's seat. When he got in the Jeep he noticed a picture she had on her dashboard. It was a picture of her and Snacks in

Times Square. "I can't believe this shit" he said to himself. "This O'l boy bitch, I'm definitely not taking no for a answer now.

"You know how to get to Central Avenue?" she said drunkenly.

"I sure do baby don't worry I got you."

"Okay if I doze off, when you get to Central Avenue wake me up so I could show you the rest of the way" Reema said before she passed out.

Qua had been slipping Ruthies in her drink all night and they finally hit her. 15 minutes later Qua pulled up to Rocky's aunt house on South park street in Elizabeth. He parked in her driveway and got out the car. He climbed the stairs of the front porch 2 at a time. He rang the doorbell like a mad man. Rocky finally answered half sleep "What da fuck you ringin the bell like you crazy for." Rocky swung the door open mad he had been awaken from his sleep.

"Fuck all that open the back door for me I got somebody with me."

Rocky slammed the door and when to open the back door. He knew the routine already this was how the entered the house whenever they had a new piece of pussy with them. Qua went to get Reema out the jeep. He opened the passenger door and struggled to get her out. "Damn you heavier than a motha fucka." He said to an unconscious Reema when he had finally got her over his shoulder. Reema mumbled something back but she was so out of it he couldn't understand it, it didn't matter to him anyway.

Rocky had opened the door and went back up stairs. Qua stumbled his way all the way to the basement. Finally reaching his destination he plopped Reema down on the futon. When he stepped back to admire his work he able to look straight up Reema's dress. "Damn baby that pussy fat." Qua s licked his lips. "I'm have to taste that" he said get on his knees spreading her legs. Her pussy was clean shaven and so enticing. Qua couldn't help but dive in face first. After a while Reema still out of started to moan. The fact that she started to moan excited Qua and got him hard instantly. He stopped eating her pussy and rammed his dick in her so hard that she started to come out of her drug induced coma. "What the fuck are you doing?" She struggled beneath him.

"Hold up don't move. I'm bout cum. He grunted as she tried to fight her way from the bottom. Qua pulled out and came all over her dress. "Damn that shit was good as hell" He said out of breath.

"Nigga you just raped me!!" She screamed and tried to rush him. He punched in the face knocking her back on the futon.

"Bitch you know you wanted it" he said standing over her pulling up his pants fixing his belt. Reema looked like she wanted to try him again and he read the look in her eyes. "Bitch you get up and I'ma Beat dat ass." Qua threatened. He walked up on her like he was about to strike her with both of his fist closed. Reema thought he was about to hit her again, so she balled up with her knees to her chest and her arms covering her head and face. "That's what I thought". Now that we got an understanding I shouldn't have no more problems out of you" He said cocky as can be. He reached out to touch her face and she rushed him. What a mistake on her behalf. When she rushed him he side stepped her and unloaded a flurry of punches on her knocking back down. Qua looked like he boxing in Kurt Center the way he moved on Reema. She cried as loud as she could. "Shut da fuck up bitch." He said kicking her in the face.

All the noise caused Rocky to come in the basement. "What the fuck you doing down here." Rocky asked entering the basement. He recognized Reema's face soon as he saw her, but from where he didn't know. He tried to rush to her aid but Qua stopped him. "Nah leave her."

"What you mean leave her?? Look at what you did" He said pointing to a battered Reema.

"When my husband find out about this your dead" she yelled between sobs.

"Fuck your husband bitch this ain't Newark. He don't run shit out here" Qua screamed in her face. She was shocked Qua spoke like he knew who her husband was.

"You know my husband?" She sniffled.

"Yeah I know that bitch ass nigga"

"If you know my husband then you know when he finds out about this you're dead" Qua went to punish her for her disrespect but Rocky held him back.

"Who is her husband?" Rocky questioned.

"Ya mans that's who."

"Who the fuck is my mans?"

Qua snapped. "Snacks nigga ya mans Snacks,"

Rocky knew Qua was crazy but he didn't think he would go this far and his face showed his surprise.

"That's right I got his bitch, and he gon pay to get her back.

"I can't believe you nigga. You brought her here, now got me in the middle of your bullshit." Rocky said as he punched the wall and walked out the basement.

"You mind as well get paid too!!" Qua screamed at Rocky's back as left the basement.

It had been close to a week since Qua had kidnapped Reema. He had been raping her repeatedly. It had gotten to the point where her started sodemnizing her. Reema's asshole was ripped open. Her eyes were swollen shut her and lips were busted. Reema was really fucked up, but this didn't stop Qua from raping her. She didn't even fight back anymore. She just laid there hoping he would finish quick. The first time Qua went into Reema's ass she shitted on him thinking that would make him stop. What a mistake! After he finished, he beat her for 30 minutes with a wire hanger. Reema had stopped praying that the torture would stop now she prayed God would just take her life.

Snacks was starting to get worried Reema wasn't even answering the phone for Neesha. No matter how upset she was at him, she would never not answer the phone for Neesha. Snacks decided to go by the house and see if she was okay. Snacks pulled up to Reema's house and something just didn't feel right. He use his key to get in when he walked in he flicked the living room lights on. Everything was in place. It didn't look like anything happened to her in the house. Snacks searched the house looking for anything that could point him in the right direction. Snacks decided to ask Mrs. James the next door neighbor had seen Reema lately. When Snacks left out the house to go next door he noticed that there was a stack of mail in the mail box, this let him know that Reema had not been home because she always checked the mail. As Snacks made his way to Mrs. James house his phone vibrated. He looked at his phone and saw it was Qua calling him." You calling me you must got the paper. "Snacks spoke into the phone.

"I think you might wanna to tone it down with all the tough shit nigga."

"You must a bumped your fucking head." Qua cut him off "No nigga I aint bumped my head but I do have something you want nigga."

"Fuck is you talkin about" Snacked asked getting angrier by the moment.

"How can I put this? Remember state property when Dame Dash called Beans? I got you bitch nigga." Qua and laughed.

"I swear to God." Snacks started but Qua cut him off again.

"I know, I know, if I touch her you gonna kill me Blah blah blah. Lets make one thing clear. You are not running shit I am mother fucka. Now I want 250 stacks in one week or this bitch is dead." Qua hung up.

Snacks was mad as a raging bull. He wanted to break something. He sat in his car and said a prayer, praying that he could get Reema back. Reema voice played in Snacks head. "When karma comes knocking on your door. I don't want to be nowhere around." Damn Bae! I'm sorry I'm coming just hold on.

Snacks first call he made was to Newarky. When Newarky picked up he heard the urgency in Snacks voice. Whatever it was Snacks wanted to talk to him about must have been important because he told Newarky he needed to meet his ASAP. Newarky told Snacks he as busy but Snacks told him it was a matter of life and death. 15 minutes later they met at White Castle on Elizabeth Ave in Newark.

"So what's so important?" Newarky asked getting in Snacks car.

"Qua snatched Reema." Snacks said almost crying.

"What do you mean Qua snatched Reema?"

"EXACTLY what I said, da nigga got my wife." Snacks was furious. "I want that nigga head" Snacks yelled pounding the arm rest. "He talking about he wants 250 stacks."

"What!!" Newarky asked. "Man that nigga crazy." He thought for a minute." He don't know Reema my cousin, so this might work for us."

"That's the first thing good I head all day." Snacked admitted.

"Have you heard from Rocky?" Newarky asked.

"Come to think about, nah he should've gotten with me by now too." Snacks said getting suspicious.

"I bet you that nigga knows something." Newarky said dialing Rocky's number.

"Yo!" Rocky answered on the first ring.

"What's up nigga?" Newarky asked.

"Same shit what up with you?"

"Where ya man at?"

"Who you talking about?" Rocky questioned.

"Don't get dumb on me my nigga. Where Qua at?"

"Look Newarky I aint fucking with dat nigga. He drugged her up talking about she was Snacks bitch I ain't want no parts so I left."

"Where he at?"

"He got her tied up in my aunt's basement."

"Why you ain't call and tell me "Snacks finally spoke." Don't get quiet now why you ain't tell me?"

"I knew you was gonna kill us both."

"Whatever nigga you a dead man." Snacks threatened. Just as Newarky hung up.

10 minutes later, after doing 100 MPH all the way to South Park St. Newarky and Snacks pulled up to Rocky's Aunt house. Snacks heart dropped when he seen Reema's truck. "That's her truck right there" he said almost jumping out the truck while it was moving.

"Don't pull in the drive way. Park up the block" Newarky instructed.

"Why not" Snacks asked.

"Just in case shit gets ugly. Nobody will know what we came in."

"You right" Snacks admitted knowing shit was going to get ugly if anybody was in the house.

As they got out the car Newarky led the way knowing how shit was layed out. They both felt it was best if he led. Snacks followed Newarky to the back of the house. Newarky tried the back door but it was locked. With one kick the fragile door flew off the hinges. Newarky and Snacks both had their guns drawn as Newarky led the way down to the basement. When they entered the basement it stunk like piss and shit. Snacks spotted Reema in the corner. She was out cold. He rushed to her while Newarky checked around for Qua. Snacks had to break the radiator to get Reema loose. She as in and out of consciousness. Mumbling something he couldn't understand. As he picked her up Newarky came running down the stairs." Yo he just pulled up, how do you want to do this?" He put Reema down on the futon and hid behind the door. Newarky turned the rights out and hid on the other side of the room. Qua came walking down the steps.

"Who the fuck came down here" he said noticing the door was cracked as he reach for the lights switch. Snacks rushed him just as the lights came on. The blow Snacks delivered with his P90 broke Qua's nose again. He screamed as blood splattered the wall. Newarky grabbed Qua from behind allowing Snacks to disarm him.

"You bitch ass nigga" Snacks yelled as he beat Qua with his own gun like a slave that had run away and been caught. When Qua hit the floor Newarky and Snacks stomped him repeatedly. Snacks spotted a bat in the corner and grabbed the bat. "Hold up. Back up my nigga got this" Snacks said moving Newarky to the said. He attacked Qua viscously with the bat. He broke every bone in Qua's body starting with his legs. "Newarky take her to her car. Pull down the streat where we parked. I'll be right behind you." Snacks turned back to Qua after giving Newarky instructions. Qua was out cold hanging on to life by a thread. Snacks picked up the gasoline can there in the corner used to fill up the lawn mower." I told you bitch ass nigga. You was a dead man". Qua tried to speak, but Snacks silenced him, pouring gas in his face." I know blah blah blah, fuck me and all that other good shit." He struck a match and laughed." When are you nigga going to learn? When I say something I mean it." He struck the match and threw it in Qua's face. The match ignited a flame that spread through the basement at a rapid pace. Snacks ran up out of there to his care like a track star. "We taking her UMD." He yelled to Newarky as they sped off and Newarky followed.

Reema had been admitted to the hospital. They ran multiple test on her for S.T.D's and other things. Snacks hadn't left her side. He stayed at the hospital 24/7. He hadn't eaten or got a good night's sleep since they arrived. Reema was in a deep sleep. She hadn't been awake not once since they'd been there. Snacks was worried, but the doctor assured him that the sleeping she was doing was good for her. A day or so later her test results proved to be negative for all S.T.D's. However she suffered a broken collar bone, her eyes were swollen shut, and she had to get 7 stitches in her anus. Snacks was hurt Reema was laid up in the hospital on the account of one of his enemies. The fact that he killed Qua didn't make him feel any better. For what Qua did Snacks felt he deserved to die a thousand deaths. His thirst for blood wasn't quenched. He needed to find Rocky. He felt like it was partly Rocky's fault for not calling him immediately when he found out she was his wife. With Qua dead and no one else to blame he turned his anger towards Rocky.

# CHAPTER 24

S HEED HAD JUST gotten back to Jersey when he received a call
from his cousin explaining he was on the run. When he initially
received the call from Rocky saying he was on the run he thought
he was running from the police but when he said he was running from
Snacks Sheed had enough. Snacks was causing too many problems.
He had ran to Atlanta to flee Snacks and now his cousin was running
from the same nigga. Enough was enough. If Rik couldn't finish Snacks
it was time he stood up and showed Snacks his gangsta wasn't to be
slept on.

Sheed knew he would need help to go war with Snacks so Rocky
having a situation with him worked perfectly. This gave him some much
needed man power. His next move would be to holla at Rah to see if
he would ride with him. While he was away he heard Rah was now
rocking with snacks and his team. Sheed knew he had a chance to get
Rah back on his squad because their relationship was closer than the

relationships he had with both Snacks and Rik. Sheed knew he had to get to Rah while he was by himself, so on his first night back in town he sat down the street from Rah's apartment hoping to catch him that night. He sat on Rah's block until the wee hours of the morning before deciding to try and catch him later. Next he would try and get with Rocky to see where his head was at. To his surprise when he finally got Rah and Rocky together they both where eager to get Snacks out the way. They all agreed that the sooner they got rid of Snacks the better.

Reema still hadn't woke up. She was heavily sedated, Snacks didn't want to leave her but Amanda told him that he at least needed to come home and eat a hot meal, take a shower, and rest a little. He also needed to tell Neesha something because she was worried sick about her mother. Amanda didn't think it would be a good idea to tell Neesha that her mother was raped. Instead she thought it would be better to tell her Reema was in a bad car accident.

When Snacks entered the apartment Neesha ran to him followed by Amanda.

"Daddy is my mommy ok?"

"She's still sleeping. She's banged up pretty bad from the accident." He hated lying to his daughter but he knew it was for her own good. "Besides a few broken bones she should be ok." After he hugged them both he headed to the bedroom taking off his jacket tossing it on the bed. He took his gun off his waist and placed it in the closet.

"I've missed you so much" Amanda said stepping out the bathroom after running the shower for him.

"Thanks baby. I missed you too." He said kissing her on her forehead going into the bathroom to take a much needed shower. While he was in the bathroom his phone had been ringing off the hook. Amanda wasn't the nosey type but the way his phone was ringing she thought it might be important. When she looked at his phone she saw 3 of the calls were from Rah and 7 were from someone named Ashlee. As she held the phone in her hand 2 text came through:

YO THIS RAH YOU COULD COME THROUGH AND THAT PAPER WHEN UR READY.....

The other read:

> DON'T DUCK ME NOW. MAN UP AND TAKE CARE UR
> BABY BECAUSE I'M 2 MONTHS PREGNANT AND I'M
> KEEPING IT....

After reading the text Amanda's Heart shattered she was hurt. Her hurt turned into rage as she stormed into the bathroom where Snacks was just getting out the shower. "Who the fuck is Ashlee?" She questioned with tears in her eyes.

"What are you talkin about?" He played dumb at the same time keeping his cool.

"Not what, but who. And you know who I'm talking about." The fact that he was playing stupid made even more upset.

"Please not now." He said wrapping a towel around his waist and brushing past her.

"Don't you fuckin walk past me. Answer me!!!" She screamed.

"She works the table for me" He down played the situation while getting dressed. He wanted to put some distance between them quick.

"Oh she's more than a table worker" She said as she pointed his phone in his face.

"So that's what we're doing now? You checkin my phone now? I can't believe you." He tried to flip it on her.

"Me? You can't believe me? Some bitch calls your phone talking about she's pregnant, and can't believe me?"

Amanda's revelation had Snacks shocked. He had slipped up and slipped up bad. Before he knew it she threw the phone at him. He managed to catch it clumsily. Just as he caught the phone she rushed him knocking him on the bed. As they landed on the bed she threw a bunch of punches all landing on his chest. He had never seen this side of her. He manage to get on top of her pinning her down.

"Mommy it's not what you think. I'ma fix this" he promised.

"Get the fuck off me" she was crying and screaming at the top of her lungs. Neesha busted in the room.

"Stop fighting! What are yall doing?"

"I'm sorry Neesha" Amanda apologized.

"No I apologize I'ma just leave" Snacks said going toward the closet to get his gun.

"No you're not going anywhere! Running isn't going to fix anything."

"I'm not running" he defended himself.

After several attempts trying to get past her to get to the closet he gave up and left out the room. Amanda figured he was only going to the living room. She hadn't knew he left the house until she heard the front door slam. She still thought very little of him leaving because he never went too far without his gun. Snacks made it to his car and just sat there for a moment staring at his phone with disbelief. The text messages from Ashlee turned his life upside down in no time at all. He contemplated on calling Ashlee and confronting her but instead he called Rah to pick his money. Rah answered immediately "Yo what up?" Snacks asked.

"You know the shit!" Rah replied cooly. "I got the bread from the last couple of days. You wanna come through and get that."

"You at the crib?" Snacks questioned.

"Yeah I'm at the crib."

"A'ight I'll be there in 15 minutes."

"A'ight hit me when you outside."

"Bet" Snacks said before hanging up.

## 20 Minutes Later

Snacks pulled up to the building on Summit and Walnut in East Orange. He dialed Rah's number.

"You outside?" Rah asked.

"Yeah I'm out here" Snacks confirmed.

5 minutes later Rah came walking out the building. Instead of Snacks letting him in the car as usual, he got out the car wanting to get some fresh air. As he got out the car he noticed someone step out the alleyway across the street. He turned to see who it was and realized it was Sheed. From Sheed's presence he knew it was a set-up, from the corner of his eye he seen Rah reach under his shirt for his gun. Snacks

first instinct was to reach for his but the argument with Amanda caused him to leave his gun home. He turned his attention back to Rah and was faced with the barrel of Rah's pistol. He took off before Rah or Sheed could get a shot off. Snacks didn't get far before Sheed hit him in the leg with his Glock 17. Snacks fell to the ground but his adrenalin got him back on his feet quickly. As he ran pass parked cars, bullets from booth Rah and Sheed's guns shattered windows and set off car alarms. Snacks thought he would get away when he made it around the corner but it was like Rocky appeared out of thin air. Rocky hit Snacks twice in the stomach with his P89. Snacks fell to the ground clutching his stomach. Rocky unloaded 5 more shots in him before Sheed turned the corner in Snacks' car. "Come on Nigga" Sheed waved him over. He shot Snacks one more time in the face before jumping in the car with Sheed and Rah "1 down 2 more to go.

Reese had been putting in overtime in the building since Snacks had been at the hospital with Reema every day. He was almost out of work and Snacks wasn't answering his phone. Reese started to wonder was the stress of everything that was going on becoming too much his man to handle. Whatever was going on he needed to speak with Snacks. Just as he was caught up in his thoughts Jeff called him out the window. "Yo Reese. Snacks turning in the projects right now." "Reese stuck his head out the window.

"Stop him and tell him to wait I'm coming down." As Jeff flagged down the Lincoln he couldn't really make out who was in the car but it looked like more than just Snacks.

"Yo Reese"

"I'm coming" Reese responded.

"I'm not sure but this don't look like Snacks in this car."

"What you mea----" Reese stopped mid-sentence because when stepped out the building, the window to the Lincoln came down and guns started firing. Reese ran back into the building as bullets just missed him. He managed to make it to a girl named Vicky's house. Jeff wasn't so lucky he got hit about 5 times and was now laid out in front of the building lifeless. "Damn who da fuck was that? And how da fuck did they get Snacks car." A million different questions was running through his head. He immediately called Beef. He told Beef everything that had just went down Beef tried to make sense of everything he just heard but nothing was adding up.

20 minutes later they linked up and cruised the city looking for any sign of their comrade. It wasn't until they found his car burned to a crisp that they started to worry. When it seemed like they were on the verge of losing their minds Amanda called. She told them that she had just received a call from a detective saying Snacks had been shot and was in U.M.D fighting for his life.

# CHAPTER 25

*15 Minutes Later*

AMANDA ALONG WITH a long with a hysterical Neesha sat in the waiting room waiting for the doctor to deliver the news. Amanda wanted to leave Neesha home but she refused to sit around while her father possibly could be dying. As Amanda paced the floor back and forth, Beef and Reese rushed in.

"What they say?" Beef questioned. Neesha ran to her uncle hugging him.

"We're still waiting" Amanda said with tears in her eyes. "The detectives left but they said they'll be back if he makes it out of surgery" she said sniffling.

"What they mean if he make it?" Reese screamed. Just then the doctor came walking into the waiting room.

"I take it you're here for Mr.Benson."

"Yes we are" Amanda spoke up grabbing Neesha by her side.

"Well Mr.Benson is a strong guy. He had some really bad injuries but he's made it through the most difficult part of the surgeries." Everybody in the room let out a deep breath. The doctor continued "We'll still have a few more things to do but he will make it. Mr.Benson suffered a shot to the jaw. He's a lucky man that whoever did this didn't manage to shoot him in the head. When we're finished I'll come back out and let you know when you can see him."

"Thank you for saving my father" Neesha hugged the doctor still crying a bit.

"Your dad is a strong guy. He fought as much as I did to save him." They all gave the doctor their thanks before he left. No one wanted to leave until they saw Snacks. It was like the time was moving in slow motion. Neesha was sound asleep with her head on Amanda's lap. Amanda was half sleep herself while Beef and Reese both paced back and forth they were all in their own thoughts when Pedro came walking in the waiting room.

Neither Beef nor Reese was familiar with the tall Spanish man. When Amanda jumped up and yelled "Daddy!" They were all aware of who he was. After she hugged him, he told her he was not there to see her but in Need to speak to Beef and Reese. She sat back down and let the men talk. They sat huddled in the corner and didn't talk above a whisper. At the end of their meeting he shook both of their hands and then walked over to Amanda and Neesha. He bent down and kissed Neesha on her cheek and spoke softly "You have been through so much in a short time but even as a young female you have the same look in your eyes as your father."

"And what look is that?" Neesha asked.

"The look of a warrior" he said before leaving. Neesha loved the fact that Pedro saw her father in her, Snacks was her biggest hero.

After the meeting with Pedro, Beef and Reese learned that Rah linked up with Sheed and Rocky and were responsible for what happened to Snacks. They also had the addresses of all 3 of their family members and closest friends. Things were about to get bloody. Amanda knew whatever Pedro told them was serious because whatever it was got them up out of the hospital and back on the streets. She knew things were about to get bad for someone. *Really! Really Bad!* She thought.

# CHAPTER 26

REEMA HAD AWAKEN sometime in the middle of the night. Her body was sore all over. She kept having visions of Qua raping her over and over again. She looked on the table in front of her and saw a newspaper article alongside a note someone had left. Inspecting the note further she realized it was from Snacks. The note read:

*Hey sleepy head,*

*I know you're in pain right now so don't worry too much about the things that has happened. I took care of EVERYTHING. I'm sorry I allowed this to happen. Please forgive me. Neesha is fine don't worry about her. I'll be back soon, I went home to take a shower and change clothes.*

*I Love You,*
*Snacks*

After reading the note she read the article. It was about Qua, she recognized him from the picture at the top of the article. One look at his face sent chills down her spine. The article said he had burned to death in a house in Elizabeth. The article also stated that an elderly lady died in the fire as well. This must be what Snacks meant when he said he took care of EVERYTHING she thought as she got up to flush the note and article down the toilet. She winced in pain as she got out the bed from being laid up all that time her body was stiff.

Amanda didn't really know what to expect when she approached room 322 in U.M.D., hopefully if Reema was woke they could talk like adults. She walked in to find an empty bed. Seconds later she heard the toilet flush letting know Reema must have been the bathroom. When Reema finally came limping out the bathroom she looked like she had been in a boxing match with Mike Tyson.

Reema saw Amanda and immediately snapped. "What the fuck are you doing in my room? And where is my husband?" Amanda threw her hands up like she surrendered.

"I come in peace" Amanda said while lowering her hands.

"Nah fuck dat get out my room!!!" Reema said grabbing the door knob. Amanda put her hand on the door preventing her from opening it.

"We need to talk."

"Bitch you musta bumped yo head." Reema continued to be disrespectful. "Get out!!!" She shouted and pointed to the door. With no other choice Amanda blurted out.

"Terrell got shot!!!" Reema grabbed her chest like she was having a heart attack. Her eyes started to water immediately. She was crying hard before Amanda could tell her that he was still alive. "Please have a seat so we can talk please." Amanda practically begged. Reema looked at her briefly before finally taking a seat on the edge of her hospital bed.

"Is he.... Is he..." Reema couldn't bring herself to ask if he was dead.

"No he's still with us but he's hurt pretty bad."

"Where's my daughter?' Reema questioned still crying.

"Ever since they let us visit him she won't leave him. We didn't tell her what happen to you. We decided-----" Reema cut her off.

"What do you mean we? He letting you make decisions when it comes to my daughter now?"

"Well, I thought it would be best for you to tell her your story when you felt the time was right. I didn't think it would be wise to tell her something so brutal, so I thought it would be best if we told her you were in a car accident. Reema thought for minute and was thankful Amanda had done what she did.

"Thank you." Reema said bowing her head humbly. Amanda reached out and lifted Reema's head with her index finger. "You have nothing to be ashamed of."

"Why are you being so nice?"

"Because right now Terrell needs us and Neesha needs us. And more importantly I'm not going to be fighting you over a man that has no control over who his heart loves. I know and understand that he loves you, but you have to realize that we have something special too. It might be a hard pill to swallow but it's real."

"You're right." Reema finally agreed. If Amanda could be grown about the situation she could too. Before they knew it they were hugging and crying together.

"Thanks I needed that." Reema admitted before finally letting go.

"Me too, me too." Amanda confirmed

# CHAPTER 27

S AV SAT BEHIND the wheel of the stolen 2014 Ford Sho he was driving for Beef and Reese. When he heard about what happen to Snacks he insisted on riding with them when they called for a car. They were a little hesitant at first but Sav Being Reese's homie he cosigned for him so Beef let him come along. Not to mention Beef knew how close Sav was to his brother so he granted him the opportunity to ride. The car was filled with smoke as they rode on their mission. They rode listing to the sounds of 2 Pac's Against all odds, and smoking some of the strongest haze on the East coast. Before heading out on their mission they went to New York on 156th street and copped the fine grade of haze.

As they approached their destination they all checked their weapons to make sure they locked and loaded. Sav pulled directly in front of the big green house in Hillside, New Jersey. Beef got out the car and climbed the steps to the house two at a time then he rang the doorbell twice. He impatiently waited for someone to answer the door just as he was about to ring the bell again he heard someone on the other side unlocking the door. "Yes young man how may I help you?" The elderly man who looked to be in his late 60's or early 70's asked peeking from behind the door. Beef stood at the door with his hands behind his back.

"Yes sir. Is Raheem home?" Beef spoke politely calling Rah by his government name like he wasn't there to bring death to Rah and whoever else he could. Rah's father sensed danger immediately upon hearing his son's name. He knew whatever his son was involved in had made it to his door step. The old man looked over Beef's shoulder and saw two other young men waiting in the car and knew this wasn't a social call. Rah's father didn't even bother to answer Beef's question instead he tried to shut the door in his face. Beef stopped the door from shutting by sticking his foot in the doorway. "Not so fast old man." Beef said forcing his way into the house.

"We don't want any trouble." The old man spoke trembling with fear. Beef pulled his 357 automatic from his waist and raised at the old man's head. The old man saw the gun and tried to scream but Beef silenced him with a single shot to the face killing on instantly. By this time Reese had made his way into the house.

"You take up stairs, I got down here." Beef pointed to the stairs with his gun directing Reese up stairs.

Soon as Reese made it up the stairs the first room he checked he caught Rah's brother with his paints down literally. When he busted in the room Rah's brother was standing in front of the T.V watching porn masturbating Reese walked up directly behind him and shot him once in the head ending his life.

While Reese was up stairs Beef searched the basement finding Rah's uncle sleeping like a baby Beef didn't bother to wake him he just shot him in the head too. The neighbors next door heard the gun shots and called the cops. Reese had already made it back to the car when Beef came running out the house.

Just as he got in the car a Hillside police car tried to box them in. At that moment Sav sprang into action. He threw the Sho into gear and took off at top speed heading towards Chanclor Ave Hillside gave chase radioing for back up. It wasn't long before Hillside and Irvington police were behind them. Once Sav made it to Chanclor Ave he made a right swinging into the inter section wildly he lost control of the car for a moment but quickly straightened the car out and took off again down the Ave. His plan was to make to the highway. If he made it to rout 78 he would surely get away. As they got close to stop light by Wendy's and the old Vally Fair the traffic was congested. With Hillside and Irvington police behind them Sav couldn't afford to slow down. He pulled within inches of a bus that was causing all the traffic. Coming close enough to hit the back of the bus at the last second he jumped on the sidewalk almost hitting a teenage boy getting on the bus. The boy dove in the bus like it was a pool of water on a hot summer day. Beef closed his eyes and braced himself for impact while Reese's eyes grew wide as baseballs. Beef nor Reese could believe he had made it through the tight spot without crashing. neither could the police because the move Sav just pulled caused the Hillside cop to crash into the back of the bus and the Irvington cop to crash into the back of the Hillside cop leaving Sav to escape without further chase.

Sav was amped up. "Wooooo!!! Ya'll niggas seen that. Nobody could fuck wit me when it come to this driving shit." It was like he took a shot of adrenaline. Once they had gotten away safely and switched cars Sav clowned Beef and Reese about how scared they were during the chase. Before they parted ways Beef made sure Sav knew how important it was that he not only got rid of the car, but he told him to burn the car so it would be no way that car could lead back to any of them.

Sav was so in love with speed and power of the Sho that after he dropped Beef and Reese off he never burned the car like he was instructed to instead he parked it he parked it in his aunt's backyard for later use.

# CHAPTER 28

**A**FTER KILLING RAH'S family Reese felt it would be a good idea if they laid low for a while. Beef was totally against it. Pedro had made clear that there would be no dope until the ones responsible for Snacks being laid up in the hospital were dead. While Beef and Reese were both in disagreement, Sav on the other hand was down for whatever. He just wanted to earn his stripes. Beef persuaded Reese by arguing that a man like Pedro didn't just fuck with anybody and even though they were close to Snacks that they should take Pedro fucking with them directly as a blessing. Snacks would be out of commission for who knows how long so they needed to keep things rolling and even if it took murdering a whole city it didn't matter to Beef one bit.

2 Days later they on the hunt again. Sav had come through with the wheels again. He pulled up on Beef's block in a 2015 rt Dodge Darango. After picking Beef up they went to pick Reese up from down

the projects. The trio searched the city high and low finding no trace of Sheed, Rah or Rocky. They still held a trump card though. They learned from Pedro that Sheed and Rocky's grandmother lived in a senior citizen's building on West Kenny Street. This was their next stop.

Once they arrived at the building they paid the maintenance man to let them in the side door so they could enter the building undetected by the cameras. They knew that every Sunday Rocky would stop by and drop off money so his grandmother to go to bingo, they hoped this week would be no different. Before knocking on the door to apartment 4D Reese covered the peephole with his index finger. He placed his ear to the door to see if she was in the apartment alone. After listening for a few seconds he turned to Beef and whispered. "She in there by herself." He knocked three times. KNOCK, KNOCK, KNOCK. Moments later grandma opened the door without bothering to try and look out the peephole. She simply opened the door and headed back to the couch to finish watching her soaps.

"You're early today. Did you bring my Pepsi like I asked?" She asked with her back turned thinking she was talking to Rocky. Beef entered the apartment last locking the door behind them. When she didn't receive an answer she turned around and was greeted by Reese aiming his 357 at her.

"Don't make a sound. Take a seat." He ordered. She obeyed his orders sitting on the couch trembling in fear. She had never seen a gun in real life she was so scared she pissed on herself.

"Please don't hurt me. I have money in my room."

"Shhh" Reese put his finger to his lip. We won't hurt you. Just answer the questions truthfully and you'll be ok." He promised. "When is Rocky due to be here?" Reese questioned the old lady while Beef looked out the window watching for Rocky to pull up.

"He should be here within the next hour." You could tell she was shaken by the way she spoke.

"Ok you're doing good. Next question. Dose Rocky have a key?"

"No" She responded shaking her head from side to side. As Reese continued to interrogate the petrified old lady there was a knock at the door.

"You expecting anybody besides Rocky?"

"No" She answered again.

"Be quiet." Reese warned her. Beef looked through the peephole holding the door knob.

"It's him." Beef whispered looking over his shoulder. Beef quietly unlocked the door. Rocky knocked again before trying the knob he knew his grandmother would sometimes leave the door unlocked when she was expecting him. Soon as he stepped through the door Beef was on him like flies on shit.

"What da fuck?" Was all he was able to get out before he was hit up side his head with Beef's gun. The smack up side his head with the gun knocked him down. He was dizzy but he came too quickly. Realizing his grandmother was in danger all he could do was beg that her life was speared.

"Please don't hurt my grandmother." Rocky pleaded.

"Shut da fuck up." Beef clunked him again pushing in the bathroom. "Turn the T.V. up." Beef instructed Reese before smacking Rocky in the head with the gun again. He pushed Rocky over the tub he was expecting him to beg for his life but he didn't say a word. Beef shot him twice in the back of the head splashing brain matter all around the tub. At the sound of the gun grandma lost her cool.

"Lord no, not my baby!!!" She managed to utter right before she passed out.

"Let's roll." Reese said leading the way to the door.

"And leave her?" Beef pointed to grandma passed out on the couch.

"I promised we wouldn't hurt her."

"I didn't." Beef said walking over to grandma giving her a head shot too. Grandma was out cold when the shot was delivered so it was painless.

"Let me find out you getting soft on me." Beef said as they walked out the apartment closing the door behind them.

# CHAPTER 29

S AV WAS ON 5th street doing his usual when one of his homies pulled up on him. "What's crackin cuz." The passenger said while hanging out the window off the beat hoopdie.

"You know the shit." Sav said while shaking hands with his homebody.

"Let me scream at you for a minute." The passenger said getting out the car. As they talked they walked down the street. "I need a car my nigga. I know you got one laying around." Sav didn't respond right away. He was thinking about the Sho he had put up in his aunt's backyard. His homie saw he was thinking and pleaded even harder. "Come om bra. Don't do me like dat."

"I got something but it's hot already."

"I don't give a fuck I need it." His homie said with desperation.

"Ok but don't say I didn't warn you." Sav said walking the kid back to the car.

"Man fuck all that. What time you want me to come back?" Sav looked at his phone.

"It's 5 now come back around 7. Sav instructed his homie as he put his phone back in his pocket.

"You sure at 7?" The kid questioned. This time Sav picked up the kids thirstiness.

"What's up wit you? Why da fuck you actin like that?"

"Nah I'm cool." The kid tried to play it off.

"A'ight be her at 7. Sav said as they shook hands and parted ways. Something told Sav that something was funny with his homie but he nixed it off and charged it to him just being paranoid.

2 hours later Sav was riding down 5th street looking for a parking spot. Normally he would have never parked a hot car on the block but he anticipated his homie being there to pick the car up any second. "There goes a spot right up there." He said to himself. As he pulled into the parking spot a Chevy Impala raced down the one way blocking him in. "What da fuck" He tried to put the car in reverse and back out the parking spot but another car came racing down from the opposite way and blocked him in from that side. Before he knew he was being pulled out the car and thrown to the ground. "Don't move mother fucker." The Newark Auto Squad detective yelled while stomping Sav repeatedly. They cuffed Sav and and beat him for a while before putting him in the back of the squad car. They searched the stolen car thoroughly.

"We got a gun!!!" One of the officers yelled as he lifted the gun in the air for everyone to see. Sav dropped his head in defeat.

"Damn how da fuck they just come for me like that?" Sav wondered as they drove him to the precinct. What Sav didn't know was earlier that day his homie had gotten caught by the same auto squad officers that had him now. The kid agreed to set Sav up for his own freedom. He even went as far as telling them Sav was the driver in the chase with Irvington and Hillside police that made the papers days ago. They made a deal with him if he could deliver the driver of that chase they would let him go. Little did he know they had plans on using him as long as they could. The kid had sold his sole to the devil and it was nothing he could do about it now.

Sav sat in the Essex County Jail's intake area waiting to be processed in. The bumps and bruises he received from the task force was starting to ache him badly. His head was killing him, his lip was swollen, and he had a black eye the task force had really worked him over. "Madison, Madison, Madison!!!" The sheriff yelled waking Sav from his doze to be processed. Upon hearing his name Sav walked into the brightly lit room where he was finger printed and had his photo taken. As he was headed back into the small bullpen the sheriff stopped him. "Madison you have some people here to see you."

"What da fuck you mean some people want to see me?" Sav snapped. Before the sheriff could answer two F.B.I. agents walked up and grabbed him by each arm.

"We'll take it from here." The tall white agent said tighten his grip.

"I don't know what ya'll want wit me." Sav said snatching his arm away from the agent.

"We can do this two ways. The easy way or, the hard way. You choose it doesn't make a difference to me." The agent said getting a little rougher this time. Again Sav tried to resist and again he met with force. They took him to F.B.I. headquarters and beat him worse than the auto squad. They added to his injuries a few broken ribs and a broken finger. They broke him physically but they he still didn't give them any information. They tried to scare him saying if didn't cooperate he would get life. They held him for three days without feeding him once before returning him to the county. The truth was their case wasn't as strong as they made it out to be. The man that was car jacked for the Sho couldn't identify the suspect, Irvington or Hillside police couldn't place Sav as the driver and they had no DNA placing him at the murder scene, so they really didn't have a choice but to let the state keep the case for now.

When the feds grabbed Sav they asked him a bunch of questions and made a bunch of threats Sav managed to keep his cool. They asked questions about local gang members, car thieves, and then they asked about Snacks that's when things started to get scary but they really didn't know shit so Sav kept his game face on and remained cool.

Beef was walking through Woodbridge Mall when his phone rang he looked at the unfamiliar number and sent it to voicemail. Soon as he put his phone back in his pocket it rang again this time he answered he figuring whoever it was would keep calling until they got an answer. "Yo" He spoke into the phone. An automated machine came on.

"You have a pre-paid call from.

"Sav" the voice on the other end said.

"Press 1 to except press 2 for a rate quote press 3 to block---" Beef pressed 1.

"Yo bra I've been tryna call you all day." Sav was happy that Beef finally picked up.

"I didn't know this number. What the fuck you doing in da county?"

"It's a long story I'd rather not get into it over this phone. Feel me?"

"I heard my nigga.

"What up doe? Beef knew Sav needed something the way he been calling him all day.

"My bail is 250,000$ the bails bondsman said he would take 25 stacks without a payment plan. I only got 12 I need you----"

"Say no more" Beef cut him off. "I got you. Have your peoples call me, and I will drop da money off to them before I go in the house tonight."

"Good lookin bra I thought I was gonna be stuck." Sav admitted.

"Never dat my nigga we family. If I got you got it." The operator came on.

"You have one minute left before you call will be terminated."

"Bra I'ma have my mother call you tonight." Sav said just before the phone disconnected. Sav was relieved to hear he wouldn't have to be sitting in the county that long. He felt he should have told Beef what went down but he knew if he did Beef would have been mad that he didn't get rid of the car like he told him to and most likely wouldn't have gave him the money needed to make bail. He would tell him just not right now.

# CHAPTER 30

SAV'S BAIL TOOK a few days longer than expected. After being held in quarantine for about four days he finally reached population he was placed on 4-E-1. 4-E-1 was a federal pod where federal inmates were being held fighting there cases or waiting to be sent back down on violations of their probation. Due to overcrowding of the jail Essex County started mixing county and federal inmates together on the same pod.

After throwing his property on his bunk Sav headed to the dayroom where some inmates were playing chess some were playing dominos and others were playing cards while a couple busied themselves watching the latest episode of Love and Hip Hop. When Sav entered the dayroom it was like a reunion he ran into people he hadn't seen in forever; He shook a few hands as he made his way over to the card table. "Damn! What good my nigga?" The brown skinned stocky dude at the table playing spades greeted as Sav walked up.

"I'm just passing through" Sav said downplaying his situation.

"That ain't what I heard." One of the others said slamming a card on the table.

"You can't believe everything you hear, but I'm happy I ran into ya'll."

"Man, how da fuck you gon be happy to come to jail." The dude at the table named Kicc- up said looking at Sav like he was crazy.

"You know what I mean."

"Nah I don't know what you mean." Kicc- up continued to give Sav a hard time.

"Chill Kicc cut the lil homie some slack.

"What's good lil bra?" Akadoo asked taking the last book made on the table.

"I need to holla at ya'll about one of the homies." As Sav spoke he looked around to make sure it was clear to talk.

"Hold up we gonna go in my room. 10 bottom!!" Akadoo yelled to the C.O. for him to open his door. The C.O. pushed a few buttons on his computer at his desk and seconds later cell 10 on the first floor opened up. Kicc, Ak, and Sav all walked to room, once inside the room AK gave Kicc a towel to cover the window on the cell door.

"A'ight lil bra, what's up?" Ak said giving Sav the floor.

"Yo the homie G-Racks on some funny shit.

"What you mean he on some funny shit?" Kicc asked.

"He worked me for the boys."

"I don't know the lil nigga like dat but I know his family." Ak admitted.

"Hold up let me call Dela the lil nigga used to be around his way." Kicc said while taking down the window block down. He opened the door and stuck his head out the door and called for Dela. After Dela got off the phone he came to the cell to see what Kicc wanted. Once Dela was in the room Sav told them the whole story and how he was setup. After hearing the story they came to the conclusion that G-Racks would be watched closely until somebody had some paperwork on him, it was also agreed that Sav wouldn't spread any rumors on him just in case his accusations weren't true. Sav was cool with that because he believed what was done in the dark would come to the light. 2 days later Sav finally made bail.

# CHAPTER 31

REEMA HAD BEEN discharged from the hospital but you wouldn't' think so because she never left. Along with Amanda and Neesha she stayed by Snacks' bedside everyday all day. Reema left the hospital the first day she was released she went home briefly to take a shower and change her clothes after that she was glued to Snacks' bedside. Reema wasn't the only one who never wanted to leave Snacks' side she damn near had to fight Neesha to get her to go to school. Neesha would go to school and directly after school she would return right back to her father's bedside. When Snack got shot he hit his head on the concrete pretty hard causing trauma to his head that was why he was in a coma. The good news was after several cat scans the doctors that there wasn't any swelling on his brain. They said he would wake up sooner or later only good knew when.

During the time Amanda and Reema spent together at the hospital they became close. It was weird at first but eventually them being around each other so much it became normal for them. Some would say they were stupid for still loving the same man but they figured that he was going to be with both of them whether they approved of it or not so they decided to roll with it.

Amanda was getting closer to her due date. She was as big as a house. She initially been told that she was having a boy but a later doctor's visit revealed she was having twins. Amanda was so anxious for Snacks to wake up to give him the good news. She knew he wanted a son so she could only imagine how excited he would be when he found out that he would be fathering two sons instead one. Reema wasn't jealous because she didn't want any more children. She knew Snacks always wanted more children and he always tried to impregnate her but it never worked because she was secretly on the depo shot or she took birth control pills. Amanda having twins was like a burden lifted off her shoulders but whoever this new bitch Ashlee was she had to go. If Snacks thought he was going to be running around getting the world pregnant then he could have them all by himself.

It was August 5, 2015. Snacks had been in his coma for nearly 2 months. Amanda and Reema sat in the room talking about how proud they were of Neesh making it to the 10th grade when Amanda's water broke. "Oh shit!" Amanda grabbed her stomach. "I think my water broke." She tried to stand up, but the next contraction hit her hard. "Aw, aw, aw!" She grunted and sat back down.

"Don't try get up, I'm get a nurse" Reema said, running frantically into the hall, calling for a nurse. "She going into labor, she going into labor!" she was screaming at the top of her lungs. Nurses came running. "She's in here" Reema pointed them towards Amanda who was on the couch breathing heavy."

Just breathe. "One of the nurses instructed her.

"Bitch I am breathing" she yelled.

The pain was too much for her. 5 minutes later, she was being rushed to the maternity ward. She wasn't due for another month and a half. And one of the twins was kicking the shit out of her. It was like he wanted out and wanted out now. When they got her to the maternity ward and did the ultrasound, it showed that one of the twins were being choked by the other twin's umbilical cord. The doctors had to perform an emergency c-section. After being in surgery for more than 2 hours, the twins made it into the world successfully, both weighing 7 lbs even. Through the whole thing, Reema never left Amanda's side until Pedro came to see his most prized possessions, his grandsons. Reema thought she should leave to give them some privacy but Pedro insisted she stay he said they were all family now and Reema's presence was welcomed. It was something about when Pedro spoke, you listened even if you didn't want too so Reema ended up staying for a while before deciding to go back to Snack's room.

When Reema entered Snacks' room, she went into a panic. The first thing she was doctors and nurses surrounding his bed she immediately started to push her way through the crowd of professionals to see what was going on only to find Snacks sitting up in the bed like he had a bad hangover. "I love you." She said as she cried tears of joy. He tried to say it back but his throat was to dry. She got the message and shook her head and mouthed the words. "I know I know." After the doctors did what they had to do with him and cleared the room Reema was all over him. "You know you're my hero right?" Snacks smiled.

"Why wouldn't I be?"

"So cocky I see getting shot didn't change you one bit."

"It only made me more relentless. Niggas is gonna pay for this I promise." Reema knew as well as whoever shot Snacks knew they had fucked up by not killing him so it was no need to try and tell him to chill. She noticed the strange look on his face and asked.

"Baby what's wrong?""

Nothing, it's just I was having this dream that Amanda was sitting over by the window and went into labor." He said scratching his head as if he was trying to make sense of his dream.

"It wasn't a dream baby."

"You mean---"

"Yup she had two boys," He was speechless his face showed it all.

"So you and her---" Reema cut him off.

"You lucky I love you the way I do." She said as she leaned in for a kiss. "ill, you got morning breath times ten right now."

"So you got jokes uh?" He pulled her in for another kiss before she left to tell everybody Snacks was up.

Pedro had some strings pulled and had Amanda and Snacks moved into the same room. The day after Snacks had awaken from his coma he was visited by Newark's Robbery/Homicide unit. They harassed him like he was the suspect instead of the victim. They were upset he didn't cooperate with them. They told him they knew he was dirty and when he slipped up they would be right there waiting.

Since Snacks had moved into the same room as Amanda, Reema started visiting less and less. Reema tried to deal with the whole Amanda situation like an adult but she loved Snacks too much to share him with another woman. She thought it wouldn't matter to her but she couldn't handle it if she tried. Snacks noticed the shift in Reema's attitude. He knew she wasn't feeling the situation but he was stuck in between a rock and a hard place. He loved both woman but he didn't know what to do. Amanda also noticed the change in Reema. Amanda knew Reema was hurt and wouldn't be around much longer. It didn't bother Amanda a bit if Reema didn't want to be around. She secretly hoped the situation would be too much for her to handle and ran her away. That way she could have Snacks all to herself.

Today was a big day for Snacks, it was time for the doctors to take off his colostomy bag. Snacks hated that he had to wear a shit bag, so he was looking forward to today like a kid looked forward to Christmas.

Since killing Rocky and Rah's family, Beef and Reese had been laying low. Some night they hooked up and hunted for Sheed and Rah. They even stalked Rah's family funeral. Rah didn't show up because he knew they'd be waiting for him. He remembered how they caught Rik slipping at Nikki's funeral. Sheed and Rah knew Snacks wouldn't rest until he caught up with them. At first they thought they were up for the challenge of going to war with Snacks, but Beef and Reese were going too hard. Sheed came up with the idea of them going back to Atlanta until thing died down. Then when Snacks got comfortable again they would come out the dark and strike again. Rah agreed but he wanted to bust one more move before they left.

# CHAPTER 32

R EEMA HAD BEEN doing a lot of crying lately. She was lonely. She had lost her husband to his new family, Neesha had moved out and started staying with Amanda and her father. Pedro had gotten Amanda and Snacks a huge house out in Brookdale, NJ with a built in pool, 6 bedrooms, 3 and a half bathrooms and a den that they converted to a game room for Neesha. They also had a 4 car garage and a basketball court in their backyard. Reema was crushed she let Amanda slide in and steal her family away. *It's just not fair* She thought. As she got out her Jeep to go in the house a blue 2014 Chevy Impala pulled up on her. "Hey stranger" the driver spoke as he lowered the window. She was caught off guard, she hadn't seen him in a long time.

"What's up?" she spoke as she looked around nervously. He noticed how she was moving and called her on it.

"I see you still scared of that nigga."

"I'm not scared" she lied "You know you can't be coming to my house like that."

"You didn't seem to mind before" he reminded her.

"You know he was locked up" she said.

"You show that nigga to much respect! He really don't deserve you."

"And you do?" she asked with a little attitude.

"Yes, I will treat you like a queen."

"You know we can't do this" she said backing away from the car but he grabbed her hand.

"I love you" he confessed. "And you can't tell me you don't have feelings for me." She thought before answering.

"I do" she admitted.

"Well what's stopping you?" She was contemplating everything that was going on in her life right now. Neesha was with Snacks and his new family, nothing was holding her here. Snacks wanted her to share him with another woman and here it was another man wanting her all to himself, why should she have to settle?

"We can't do it here, and you know that. Snacks will never let us be happy." she reminded him.

"We don't have to. I'm leaving in a few days and I want you to come with me so we could start a life together.... Just me and you." A tear dropped from her eye, she was confused at the moment but one thing for sure... she didn't want to be a part of Snack's love triangle. "Just think about it. I'll call you in a few days when I'm ready" he said as he kissed her and sped off leaving her stuck between a rock and a hard place.

## Days Later

Snacks had been released from the hospital. They moved into the house and everything seemed to be going great. Everything except his relationship with Reema. She wouldn't answer any of his calls or return any of his texts. Today was Neesha's last day at Central High before she started at her new school in Brookdale on Monday. Snacks told her he would be there to pick her up but she begged him to let her spend some time with her friends on her last day. Neesha always knew how to get what she wanted from her dad.. she was his weakness.

Rah sat parked in a stolen Ford Explorer waiting on school to let out. When the bell rang the teenagers came pouring out the school. Rah sat up anxiously waiting on his target. Neesha was so engaged with her friends she never saw Rah pull and shooting out of the SUV. Rah pulled up to the crowd of teenage girls and let his Glock17 rip recklessly.

*"Boom! Boom! Boom! Boom! Boom!"*

After he let off 5 shots he sped off. When he made it to safety he called Sheed. "Bra you still leaving tonight" he questioned.

"Yeah I'm out soon as I pick up my peoples" he confirmed.

"Ok cool I'ma get my own rental and I'll be right behind you."

"Ok bra don't play up here too long" Sheed warned him.

"I'ma be right behind you. Don't worry."

Amanda came rushing into the room, she grabbed the remote and flicked to the news. Snacks tried to protest but when he saw the reporter was talking about a shooting that had taken place at Neesha's school he became very attentive.

*"Hi, I'm Nancy Peters reporting to you live from Central High School in Newark, Nj where 3 teenage girls have been shot. 2 pronounced dead on the scene. The other wounded and taken to U.M.D. it's a tragic day here in Newark. I'M Nancy Peters reporting to live from Central High School back to you Jim.*

Snacks immediately dialed Neesha's number. When he got no answer his heart skipped a beat. After dialing Neesha's he tried Reema. In days she still hadn't responded to him Snacks was heated when she didn't answered now wasn't the time for her to be in her feelings for all he knew Neesha could be dead. He was on the verge of a nervous breakdown.

Reema looked back at her house one last time before getting in the car. Tears ran down her face as she put her luggage in the trunk. As she got in the passenger seat she took a deep breath and exhaled as she closed the door. "You ready?" her new found love asked as they pulled off. It felt nice to be cared for even if it wasn't by Snacks. "You know I love you right?"

"I love you too. Sheed" She said as she leaned over and kissed him. She pressed send on her phone and threw it out the window. Whit the press of the button she just sent Snacks one final text. She tossed the phone out the window because she didn't want to know his response she figured he would try to talk her into staying. At this moment all she cared about was her own happiness. When she made it to Atlanta and got settled she would call Neesha but as of right now all she was worried about was her and her own happiness

Snacks looked at his phone in total disbelief as he sat in passenger seat of Amanda's car and read the text Reema just sent him.

Reema; **Don't bother to come looking for me. I'm moving on. I've found someone who will love me the way I love him. I have always been a rider for you and you never truly appreciated me. I guess now you will realize what you had now that I'm gone**.

I can't believe this shit. Snacks thought to himself. Every time things seem to be going good something always goes wrong. My daughter might be dead and this bitch running around looking for love. I can't win for losing. What am I doing wrong? Am I playing the game wrong? Am I really playing a game I can't win? Or am I really playing A Game For Fools???

To be continued.......

Made in the USA
Middletown, DE
29 January 2021

32635430R00104